ARK: ASTEROID IMPACT

BOOK 1 OF THE ARK TRILOGY

D1596114

THOMAS A. CAHILL

EditPros LLC, Davis, California, USA · www.editpros.com

Published by EditPros LLC
423 F Street, suite 206
Davis, CA 95616
www.editpros.com

ISBN-10: 1937317072
ISBN-13: 978-1-937317-07-2

Library of Congress Control Number: 2012954518

Printed in the United States of America

CATALOGING INFORMATION:

Cahill, Thomas A.

Ark: Asteroid Impact
Filing categories:
    Fiction: Science Fiction - General
    Fiction: Science Fiction - Adventure
    Fiction: Action & Adventure
    Survivalist Thriller

CONTENTS

In addition to my darling wife, Ginny, I would like to especially acknowledge my editors, Jeff and Marti, who helped turn concept into reality, and several of my friends who provided insightful comments. While the science of the disaster and the locations of the action are as accurate as I can make them, any similarities to persons living or dead are purely coincidental.

1. UNCERTAINTY

I loved early morning classes. The students were generally sharper, the temperatures cooler, and once the classes were done, the rest of the day was mine until the almost inevitable afternoon faculty meetings, departmental colloquia, and seminars – the unsung burden of all faculty. My name is Ken, and I'm a physicist and professor from Davis, in California's Sacramento Valley. I was almost bouncing back to my office after my Intro Physics class when Sheldon, probably my best friend on the faculty who handled Intro Astronomy, accosted me in the hall. His usually ebullient persona was uncharacteristically subdued. He appeared pensive – even worried.

"What's up?" I asked.

He directed me into my office, closer than his, without saying a word.

"Ken, I really feel stupid about this, and I am telling only you in the hope that you will find some other explanation."

He dumped himself into my only comfortable chair.

"What do you know about near-Earth objects?" he asked.

"Precious little, except there are some, and one of them was the source of the asteroid hit that caused the Cretaceous-Tertiary mass extinction that wiped out the dinosaurs. The crater is somewhere in the Yucatan, I believe."

"Well, as you know, I check each morning for interesting astronomical information I can use to make my class relevant, and one source is the NASA Near-Earth Object Program website. This morning, it was devoid of any information, which is in itself unusual."

"Anyway, I was scanning my e-mail messages when I saw a reply marked 'highest urgency' from Robert Gibbs, a colleague of mine at the University of Washington, who probably hit the wrong key. The message read, 'Please check again. Not 4179 Toutatis!'

"The recipients list indicated that the message had been intended for almost the entire Near-Earth Object community, and I was added by accident. I tried to call. No answer. I went to the NASA site and 4179 Toutatis was not even listed. It had been indexed there a few days ago because it was going to come close to Earth soon, like tomorrow, and within the orbit of the Moon, but it seemed to pose no real threat."

Sheldon sat, silent. "I know I will feel like a complete idiot tomorrow when it turns out someone's server was down, but...." He never finished the sentence.

We sat in silence, each working out the scenario that 4179 Toutatis might be a lot closer to an Earth impact than we recently thought.

"How big is it?" I asked.

"Something like a 10 kilometer-long dumbbell, perhaps slightly smaller than the size of the K-T asteroid," he answered.

"Well, if NASA and your colleagues are clammed up, I wonder about the military. Let's try the public information line at Beale Air Force Base. They fly all kinds of surveillance aircraft, and they might be involved if something big is up."

We both hoped for a cheery voice on the line, announcing the date of the next public air show, but nothing. The line was down. No answer, no message.

"Crap!" I said. "I don't like that one bit. What other resources do we have?"

"Let's check the White House. The president's new openness allows us to see the daily schedule," Sheldon mused.

It turned out that all meetings with the president had been cancelled about an hour and a half ago, and no rescheduling had been done. Further, all tours of the White House had been cancelled, "Due to building repair needs," said the site.

My morning coffee was cold, but I drank it anyway.

"So now we have a real choice to make. If we assume that

Toutatis strikes Earth, there will be catastrophe at the level that could extinguish essentially all land animals and our civilization. This has to be considered a finite possibility. How should we respond?"

Sheldon leaned forward, and said, "If this were to occur, what are the best chances for our survival, assuming any survival is possible?"

He continued, "The big effects would be that the Earth would ring like a bell, flex all faults, and ignite all pending volcanoes. Then the flex would generate tsunamis perhaps 3,000 feet high, maybe much more. Then there would be an eruption of volcanic fumes from the impact crater, poisoning the atmosphere. The consequence of that probably would be a massive global winter as the sulfuric acid cloud reflects away the sun, and a sharp but probably short ice age. I don't know what additional impact would come from the acid rain, but the Permian extinction was thought to have been triggered by enormous basaltic eruptions in Siberia that poisoned the atmosphere. I probably missed a few, but you get the picture."

I replied, "So to survive, one would have to be at an elevation above about 3,000 feet to avoid the tsunamis. You would have to have shelter, say a cave or mine, and enough food to last several years of brutal cold. When the weather relented, you could find an Earth possibly with much to all terrestrial life extinguished – although clearly some survived the K-T extinction, such as the small mammals from which we are descended. We would need the resources to grow our own food eventually. In the long term, that seed repository in the Arctic could be accessed to revive the Earth's flora, but for fauna...." The enormity of our scenario was starting to sink in.

I continued, "Look at this logically. As long as we don't tell anybody our suspicions, we won't be labeled nut cases when all turns out to be OK. But if we do nothing, we are toast, with all of our families and friends. I can't risk that. I propose we take a sudden vacation, like by noon, and drive north. My thoughts are that if the Earth is to survive, it is because of its oceans. They will eventually rain or snow out the pollutants, and temper the intense cold.

"We came across an old chromium mine about 250 miles northwest of Davis three years ago while exploring dirt roads in my Jeep. It is within the Six Rivers National Forest, west of Redding, and near the tiny community of Salyer. It was not far off the main road, on the side of Horse Mountain, which is about 5,000 feet high. We would be at about 2,500 feet in the mountains and only about 45 miles east of Eureka. I know the mine is locked and barred, but with a couple of winches, we could break in.

"All we are risking is a fine and repair costs, but it would be the best thing I can think of. I expect that if this impact is going to occur, the government will be doing everything it can to blow up the asteroid with ICBMs, but they'll have to let people know fairly soon. I want to be out of the area and in the mountains with all the food we can buy before that announcement is made.

"Then the questions we have are: Who should we take with us?

Who will believe us? My family is grown up, and my closest friends are the students who work for me on my projects, some of whom are close to Father John, a Jesuit priest and ex-physicist at the Newman Catholic Center in Davis. But for every person we bring, we should have enough food for two or three years. That will not be easy to do. I will e-mail my kids, and let them know my fears. I have no idea what they can or will do, but they are pretty astute."

Sheldon squirmed in his chair, almost fearing to get up and start what in all odds would be a ridiculous set of actions that surely would come back to haunt them, but logic prevailed. "I guess we have work to do."

"Wasn't that a quote from Lord of the Rings: The Two Towers by a corrupt magician? Not a good choice of words, but so be it. Let's meet at noon in the Nugget Market parking lot. I have three gas cans I will fill."

* * *

Ken looked at his familiar office, comforting and secure. The table to the right of the desk held piles of research results in the lengthy process of getting published. Books on the shelves were old friends, some going back to his graduate student days at UCLA. Class notes were piled neatly on a per-lecture basis on his bookshelves. His main computer was on and set to Google. Could this all be soon obliterated? He so wanted to just sit in his chair and have it all go away. But then he thought of his darling wife.

He grabbed his laptop computer, one obsolete but workable solar-powered Texas Instruments calculator, and an old copy of the *American Institute of Physics Handbook*, as he left. The door softly closed. He didn't bother to lock it.

2. PERIGRINATOR LEX

At about 12:20 p.m., four vehicles were in the parking lot of Nugget Market. Everybody looked enormously uncomfortable, scared, worried, uncertain, trusting Sheldon and Ken, but hoping that they were wrong. The group was very quiet, almost furtive, and kept to the far edge of the parking lot away from the crowds at the market. Ken asked everybody to hand him their cell phones and keep electronically quiet so they wouldn't all look like nut cases if it turned out to be a false alarm. It was so hard to believe that all of this – the town, the fields, the farms, the university – could be under thousands of feet of water by the next morning. Father John had called the students together using the code phrase "Perigrinator Lex," Latin for migration of the flock, which he said he lifted from *A Canticle for Leibowitz*, a post-apocalyptic science fiction novel written by Walter M. Miller Jr., that was first published in 1960. Five of the students decided to join, although Sheldon and Ken were unable to determine whether any of them took it seriously. All agreed that as soon as there was any confirmation, they would alert all their friends and suggest ways to survive the catastrophe.

Everybody hoped this was some terrible mistake and all would be normal tomorrow. The people who knew Ken and Sheldon best were quiet and worried. Still, many used the opportunity to buy staples from the market, and all vehicles were filled to capacity, including the roof racks of the SUVs. Personal gear included what you might take on a camping trip, plus some books.

Some of the students had taken the time to do their own research, and new facts were starting to appear. Anything involving satellite use had been shut down; GPS didn't work anymore. But most importantly, the president of the United States was scheduled to talk to the nation at 3:00 p.m., Pacific Daylight Time. All military bases were at the highest alert level, and the word was going out to Homeland Security personnel to terminate vacations and return to offices. Ken and Sheldon drafted a long e-mail, ready to send it to all their friends if the president in his talk confirmed their fears, but before the Internet would be incapacitated by too much traffic.

Eighteen people crammed into three SUVs and Ken's Chevy Volt, which was sort of a ridiculous car for such a journey, but it was all he had beyond his Jeep, and it had a very big battery. The hastily gathered refugee group consisted of Father John, five Newman Center students, Ken and his wife, Cathy, Sheldon and Veronica, and eight students on Ken's staff.

They drove north on Interstate 5 as a convoy, and decided to refill gas tanks and buy as much food as they could in Redding well before the scheduled national address, packing much of it in boxes and on the overloaded roof racks of the SUVs.

They were well along on state Route 299 toward Arcata when the national talk aired, almost 30 minutes late. They had pulled into a local Starbucks with Wi-Fi capabilities, and waited. They were in range of one AM station that was the designated Emergency Alert System radio outlet in the area.

"I speak to many of you, perhaps for the last time," the president began. *"An asteroid named Toutatis will strike the Earth tomorrow morning at 10:22 a.m., Eastern Daylight Time – roughly between the coast of Africa and Madagascar."*

Ken instantly hit the "Send" command on the prepared message to everybody they knew, especially warning them of the possibility of an impending and extended cold period.

"It is about the same size as the one that resulted in the extinction of the dinosaurs. We, and all nations, are deploying every weapon we have to destroy or redirect the asteroid, to reduce the disaster that will occur, but our scientists are not optimistic, considering the size of the asteroid and the short time for preparations. Normally, the asteroid Toutatis would have passed safely by the Earth, but there was slight perturbation of its orbit from an encounter a few days ago with a much smaller asteroid, and its course was changed to impact. The nature of the ensuing disaster is very uncertain, but I ask everybody to move inland from near ocean sites because tsunamis will almost certainly occur. Stock up on water and food, for there may be disruptions of services for days or even weeks. We will stay on the air to provide all new information to your emergency response radio channels.

"God bless all of you, and God bless America and the entire Earth."

In every vehicle, there was a stunned silence, as each pondered the wildly uncertain future. Any thoughts that their fears were exaggerated and their mission ridiculous vanished. As they raced for the vehicles, many got on their cell phones, but all circuits were flooded by then and no more connections were made.

Luckily, the road was good, and to their surprise, things seemed normal. Perhaps people hadn't heard, or didn't believe the president. The canyon of the Trinity River was beautiful in this late spring period, with good river flows and some dogwood in the side canyons. The road was curvy, and so their speeds had to be reduced even though their anxiousness made them want to go faster. Finally, just past the tiny hamlet of Del Loma, three cars came at high speed from the direction of Arcata. A few miles past the community of Salyer, Ken slowed and finally found an inconspicuous road to the south. There was a gate across the way that had not been there three years ago. They all stopped. Ken attached the winch to the gate and pulled, and the lock fractured without much trouble.

The group decided to have Ken's Jeep go in first, driven by Cathy, while Ken was behind in the Volt, in case the road got too rough. After all vehicles had gone through the gate, they closed it to look as secure as ever, but a close inspection would have revealed the broken lock. The road beyond was better than Ken remembered, and had been improved. The next seven miles posed no problems, even for the Volt. They arrived at the mine opening at 4:20 p.m., and not much had been changed since Ken had last seen the area. The mine was well barred, but a small shed had been built next to it.

Again Ken connected the winch to the gate of the mine, and

pulled. The main bar suddenly came loose. The mine was open, and he pushed the remaining bars aside and back.

"Let's unload immediately," said Ken. "I want to go back to that last town and buy all the provisions they will sell me. All three SUVs will come as soon as we're unloaded."

Cathy noticed Ken slipping the scope-mounted .30-06 rifle into the Jeep.

It was about 5:30 p.m. when the 18 refugees arrived at the Salyer General Store. There was little activity around it, and they went inside. The owner lounged beside the cash register. "I suppose you want supplies, too? He asked. "Well, cash only, considering the circumstances. Those other fellers seemed ticked when I wouldn't take their credit card, but things aren't normal – although, I don't believe a word the president says. I think he is starting a war so as to help him get re-elected."

Ken replied, "I've got about $1,100 in cash. How much would I need for all your food stocks?"

"A lot more than that," the store owner said.

Then Ken laid out seven coins, all gold, including two rare $20 eagle coins. "What you see is what I got – $1,100 cash and those coins."

The owner grinned, "Actually I would have given it all to you for $1,000, if you had bargained a bit. You have my whole stock. I am not sure those other fellers might be back with guns – they were not happy, so grab it while you can."

"Done. OK, team, everything, including tools and seeds."

"Wait a minute. I didn't say anything about tools!"

"OK, how about two of each, and we can scrape up another $500 from the students." Actually, the students didn't have that

THOMAS A. CAHILL

much cash, as they all use credit cards, but they produced a pretty good pile of cash, and the owner relented.

Within 15 minutes, every SUV was loaded inside and on the roof. There were a lot of canned goods, some flour and yeast, and a lot of beer and drinks were left behind. "Forget that stuff," Ken said. "We have water."

Father John piped up, "I need some bottles of red wine, and let's get some Vodka as an antiseptic."

The manager look startled, and said, "You guys are serious about this stuff!"

"Dead serious, old timer. And you should see to yourself. I think it is going to get real nasty along this road within the hour."

"Got a point, there," he said, as he started to load the whisky bottles into a large pack.

The refugees were back through the gate in 35 minutes, and re-set it. They had passed two vehicles, both going inland, but none were in sight when they turned off. They made extra efforts to hide their tracks, as they climbed up the road to the mine. When they arrived at the mine, they loaded most of the goods inside.

About an hour later, they saw smoke from roughly the direction of Salyer.

The madness had begun.

The vehicles were parked on both sides of the mine entrance facing down the road, so their lights could be used, if necessary.

"Tonight we post guard with all weapons on the ready. We have four rifles, a pistol, a sword, and assorted knives. Father John, I am excluding you, but everybody who has ever shot a gun is needed. I want you to build firing locations on both sides of the mine entrance. We'll take four-hour shifts. Either all hell

12

will break loose at 7:22 a.m. tomorrow our time, or nothing will happen.

"David, I know you are a hunter. I want you to climb above the mine, dig out a trench, and get a good sightline so we can't be easily flanked. Here is a whistle. Sound it once if flanked on the right, twice on the left, and three times for all clear. Take my .30-06. Go!"

Inside the mine, they found a newly installed electric terminal box. Ken checked. A spark confirmed that it was functioning. "Live. Plug in the Volt, and anything else that needs charging. This power will not last long, I fear. Now let's get radios on to hear what is happening. I will tune in to XM Satellite Radio in the Volt."

3. CLOSE ENCOUNTERS OF THE LETHAL KIND

The airwaves were filled with all sorts of commentary from experts and nuts alike, but official briefings were every hour on the hour, with Janet Napolini of Homeland Security as the first spokesperson. Sheldon thought they might have missed a briefing while they were running around, but they hadn't.

6:00 p.m., Pacific Daylight Time

"I am Janet Napolini, head of Homeland Security, reporting from the U.S. Naval Observatory in Washington, D.C. I am providing the 9:00 p.m. Eastern Daylight Time briefing. We have deployed every resource of every nation in an attempt to use hydrogen weapons to deflect the asteroid, but it turns out that reprogramming the trajectories into the Indian Ocean area was never in their original design. Most land-based U.S. missiles do not have enough range, and the submarine-based missiles cannot get in place soon enough

to effectively strike.

"The Russians have re-programmed a few of their largest liquid-fueled intercontinental ballistic missiles with a single massive warhead, and they will fire these aiming for an intercept at an altitude of about 120,000 feet. Their accuracy is poor, and they are triggered for an air burst at about 20,000 feet. They will try to reduce that distance, with launch at about 9:55 a.m. Eastern Standard Time.

"The speed of Toutatis will be on the order of 30,000 miles per hour, 44,000 feet per second, so 2 seconds later it will approach a squadron of B-52s armed with hydrogen bombs, flying in a circle around the trajectory of impact. These bombs will be detonated to vaporize as much of the asteroid as possible, with the brave sacrifice of hundreds of airmen who volunteered for this mission. Breaking the asteroid into pieces will cause a larger proportion of it to incinerate upon entry into the atmosphere, and less damage will occur.

"One second later, at exactly 10:22:43, what remains of the asteroid will strike the Earth in Mozambique near the city of Puerto Amelia. We are running models of potential damage, but these depend on how successful the intercepts are. All models predict massive tsunamis. We will tell you more as we learn more. God bless you all."

The intervening period was filled with civil defense information, scientists giving predictions, comments by people on the streets – many of whom declared deep skepticism of the predictions – and, occasionally, music.

9:00 p.m., Pacific Daylight Time

"I am Janet Napolini, head of Homeland Security, reporting from

the U.S. Naval Observatory in Washington, D.C. I am providing
the midnight briefing. The first part of this message will be a repeat
of the 9:00 p.m. Eastern Daylight Time briefing, followed by additional updated information.

"We have deployed every resource of every nation in an attempt
to use hydrogen weapons to deflect the asteroid, but it turns out
that reprogramming the trajectories into the Indian Ocean area
was never in their original design. Most land-based U.S. missiles
do not have enough range, and the submarine-based missiles cannot get in place soon enough to effectively strike.

"The Russians have re-programmed a few of their largest liquid-
fueled intercontinental ballistic missiles with a single massive warhead, and they will fire these aiming for an intercept at an altitude
of about 120,000 feet. Their accuracy is poor, and they are triggered for an air burst at about 20,000 feet. They will try to reduce
that distance, with launch at about 6:55 a.m. Eastern Standard
Time, for intercept at 10:22:40.

"The speed of Toutatis will be on the order of 30,000 miles per
hour, 44,000 feet per second, so 2 seconds later, it will approach a
squadron of B-52s armed with hydrogen bombs and flying in a circle around the trajectory of impact. These bombs will be detonated to vaporize as much of the asteroid as possible, with the brave
sacrifice of hundreds of airmen who volunteered for this mission.
Breaking the asteroid into pieces will cause a larger proportion of
it to incinerate upon entry into the atmosphere, and less damage
will occur.

"One second later, at exactly 7:22:43, what remains of the asteroid will strike the Earth in Mozambique near the city of Puerto
Amelia. We are running models of potential damage, but these de-

pend on how successful the intercepts are. All models predict massive tsunamis. We will tell you more as we learn more.

"Atmospheric models show a 'nuclear winter' pattern with sulfuric acid scattering light back into space, cooling the Earth. How long or how intense this effect will endure will remain unknown until we learn more about the impact.

"We have learned that the Space Station will thankfully be almost on the far side of the Earth when the impact occurs. The Russians sent up an unmanned Soyuz capsule 34 minutes ago to rendezvous with the station as a possible escape pod, if needed. It has been given an extreme orbit that will allow docking by 9:45 a.m. Eastern Daylight Time, before the impact.

"The Space Station has linked to the XM Satellite Radio network, and will be continuously broadcasting on the XM information channel.

"God bless you all."

Midnight, Pacific Daylight Time

"I am Janet Napolini, head of Homeland Security, reporting from the U.S. Naval Observatory in Washington, D.C. I am providing the 3:00 a.m. Eastern Daylight Time briefing. The first part will be a repeat of the midnight briefing, and additional information is being added.

"But first, a message from our president."

The president audibly drew in a deep breath before speaking.

"Fellow Americans, we face the potential of an almost unimaginable tragedy in just a few hours. In catastrophic situations, Americans have always risen to our highest and best citizenship. I know that with the help of your friends and the grace of God, you will so rise again. God bless you, and God bless America and the World."

Janet continued, *"We have deployed every resource of every nation in an attempt to use hydrogen weapons to deflect the asteroid, but it turns out that reprogramming the trajectories into the Indian Ocean area was never in their original design. Most land-based U.S. missiles do not have enough range, and the submarine-based missiles cannot get in place soon enough to effectively strike.*

"The Russians have re-programmed a few of their largest liquid-fueled intercontinental ballistic missiles with a single massive warhead, and they will fire these aiming for an intercept at an altitude of about 120,000 feet. Their accuracy is poor, and they are triggered for an air burst at about 20,000 feet. They will try to reduce that distance, with launch at about 6:55 a.m. Eastern Standard Time, for intercept at 10:22:40.

"The speed of Toutatis will be on the order of 30,000 miles per hour, 44,000 feet per second, so 2 seconds later it will approach a squadron of B-52s armed with hydrogen bombs flying in a circle around the trajectory of impact. These bombs will be detonated to vaporize as much of the asteroid as possible, with the brave sacrifice of hundreds of airmen who volunteered for this mission. Breaking the asteroid into pieces will cause a larger proportion of it to incinerate upon entry into the atmosphere, and less damage will occur.

"One second later, at exactly 7:22:43, what remains of the asteroid will strike the Earth in Mozambique near the city of Puerto Amelia. We are running models of potential damage, but these depend on how successful the intercepts are. All models predict massive tsunamis. We will tell you more as we learn more. God bless you all."

The intervening hours were filled with comments from spiritual heads – the Pope, Dalai Lama, and others. The music tended to be funereal classical.

3:00 a.m., Pacific Daylight Time

"I am Janet Napolini, head of Homeland Security, reporting from the Naval Observatory in Washington, D.C. with the 6:00 a.m., Eastern Daylight Time, briefing. All efforts to destroy the asteroid are in place, but as we approach the time of impact, the events will proceed so fast that no reportage will be possible. By now you should be in an area that is as secure as you can find, well away from the coast. After 10:00 a.m., Eastern Daylight Time, we will tap into all relevant informational feeds – the Department of Defense, and then NASA. We also have collaborators in South Africa and southern Indian observatories."

A repeat of civil defense information was aired along with survival preparation advice and comments about the enormous traffic jams that were occurring as citizens who finally woke up to what might happen rushed to leave coastal and low-lying inland areas.

6:00 a.m., Pacific Daylight Time

"I am Janet Napolini, head of Homeland Security, reporting from the Naval Observatory in Washington, D.C., with the 9:00 a.m. Eastern Daylight Time briefing. All measures are in place to protect key members of the government in the event of disaster. All measures are in action for the attempt to destroy the asteroid."

The rest was pretty much a repeat of previous briefings.

7:00 a.m., Pacific Daylight Time

Dawn had broken over the Klamath Mountains, and no sign of trouble had occurred anywhere near the mine site. The smoke seen last evening was no longer evident. There were no sirens or any other sounds from the highway, which was only seven miles away. Everybody was clustered around the Volt, which had the best feed from XM satellite radio.

"*I am Janet Napolini, head of Homeland Security, reporting from the Naval Observatory in Washington, D.C., with the 10:00 a.m. Eastern Daylight Time briefing. The projected time of impact is now only 22 minutes away. All measures are in place to protect key members of the government in the event of disaster. All measures are in action for the attempt to destroy the asteroid. I have been told by the Russians that almost all rockets were successfully launched toward the intercept point. I now switch over to the NASA feed, followed by the Department of Defense, as I leave the Naval Observatory and attempt to join the governmental team in a secure location. God bless us all, and God bless the United States of America.*"

She relinquished the microphone to another speaker.

"*I am Charles F. Barnard Jr., NASA administrator. We have sent aircraft into the Indian Ocean at staggered distances from the projected point of impact, repositioned the angle of the Hubble telescope to view the site, and linked to the only Earth weather satellite with a view of the area. We have confirmed the point of impact, and the fact that Toutatis will strike end on. We have also backtracked and found the point at which its orbit was perturbed. Now I turn over to the Department of Defense.*"

Amid a shuffling of papers, another speaker began, "*I am Secretary Allan Foster, and I will handle the Department of Defense reportage. First, we switch to a live feed from General Roger Arnold, son of the legendary Hap Arnold of SAC. Roger, you are on.*"

Roger Arnold began, "*On behalf of all the 124 volunteer crew members of this B-52 squadron, I want you to know that we view* this mission, which will inevitably involve our deaths, as the best and highest purpose any of us could ever imagine. Do not weep for us, for we are honored to be a key team to mitigate this catastrophe. By our actions, we hope to save billions of lives. No member of the United States armed forces could ever ask for more.

"We are flying at 28,000 feet in the tightest circle we can around the projected point of impact. The H-bombs will be automatically and simultaneously triggered by radar for the maximum effect. If any problem occurs in the radar feed, I have a manual ignition button. Any decision to switch to manual deployment will have to be done in a split second, and would result in loss of some of our ability to vaporize part of the asteroid.

"None of our predictions lead us to believe we can destroy it, for it is coming in end on and the far part of the asteroid will not absorb the maximum impact of the H-bomb fireball. Because of the timing of the departure, it was not possible for even phoned farewells from the crews. We have recorded these, and they have already been sent to family and friends. Please remember us in your prayers, and hope and pray that we may have success. I have to sign off now. God bless you all."

A good fraction of the Earth's population was now glued to the feed of the one weather satellite that had a good view of the impact site. NASA was now providing updates over both the radio and the weather satellite feed.

"I am Charles F. Barnard Jr., NASA administrator. There will be little to see before impact, because the asteroid will come in at a terminal velocity of 34,320 miles per hour – far faster than any bullet. My team and I will try to give you as much information as we can. We are now only five minutes from impact. I will stay on this open channel, and report anything of interest. But little will happen in the next few minutes."

Never had five minutes passed so slowly. Some people fainted because in their terror they forgot to breathe.

At 10:22:40, the video signal disappeared.

10:22:41 – "NASA here. Impact has occurred. All satellites swamped by intense light. We are getting no optical data."

10:22:46 – "DOD here. We received five words from Arnold – 'Bad radar, blinding light. Trigger.' We interpret that as a manual trigger."

10:22:53 – "This is NASA. South Africa reports an astounding fireball on the northeast horizon. Their comment is that it is roughly spherical, which means it is reaching up out of the atmosphere and into space. We also lost feed from the nearest SR-71 observer plane, but we are just now receiving video from the backup, which is more than 3,000 miles north of the impact site."

10:23:07 – "NASA here. Rossi X-ray Timing Explorer (RXTE) has downloaded a fast spectrum that consists of two X-ray signals at 6.4 keV, the X-ray of iron, 2.2 seconds apart. The first was about the time of the Russian intercepts, and it appears that one or more of the Russian intercontinental ballistic missiles damaged the asteroid. The second and much larger pulse was coincident with the United States' H-bomb detonation. It is so large that it appears a significant fraction of the forepart of Toutatis was vaporized. The sacrifice of the airmen was not in vain."

10:23:56 – "NASA here. India confirms the enormous fireball. The earthquake shock waves will arrive in South Africa in about eight minutes, for India 12 minutes, for the United States 32 to 40 minutes."

10:24:15 – "*NASA here. The Space Station will get its first view of the impact area in about 22 minutes. Its orbit will take it about 300 miles northeast of the impact site at the closest approach.*"

10:32:01 – "*NASA here. South Africa reports an enormous smoke and dust cloud plume heading west on the horizon, dimensions unknown. Note that is the direction that the southerly trade winds blow.*"

10:34:02 – "*I am Janet Napolini, head of Homeland Security, reporting from the Homeland Security airborne command center. The surface and pressure waves of the impact have yet to arrive in populated areas in which we still have communications. Maintain all cautions, especially for tsunami. All the models predict them.*"

10:35 – "*NASA here. We have a report from the backup SR-71 reconnaissance plane that it is being pelted by small black rocks. So far, the canopy is holding. However, no useful optical data was taken because the unexpected brightness of the asteroid and/or H-bombs saturated all sensors.*"

10:42 – "*Napolini here. CNN has relayed a panicked report from Sri Lanka about a massive tsunami 'like a mountain,' followed by collapse of all communication links.*"

10:45 – "*NASA here. South Africa is experiencing the surface wave, which is of very large amplitude but a long wavelength motion that appears to be limiting damage in Johannesburg. However, all communication has been lost with Durban, a coastal city.*"

10:52 – "*NASA here. We are getting reports of tsunami of astounding size approaching Goa on the west coast of India. Bombay is in panic, because it should arrive there in about 20 minutes.*"

10:56 – "* Napolini here. We are now getting reports of surface and pressure waves in North Africa and massive tsunami action in the Mediterranean. Johannesburg reports Capetown no longer responds. The pressure waves are about to reach the Atlantic."

High in the Klamath Mountains, the refugees were glued to the XM radio when suddenly the land underneath them pulsed and swelled like a ship on the sea. Surprisingly, little damage was done. A sense of relief started to spread among the students, but Ken and Sheldon were frozen in despair.

The middle of the North Pacific is almost exactly opposite from the point of impact. Pressure waves bounced and reflected, and thousands of miles of the seabed of the Pacific Basin flexed up by more than 100 meters – which is about 325 feet.

11:04 – "NASA here. The entire world is experiencing tsunamis that are in places thousands of feet high, essentially erasing all coastal areas of the world up to distances of hundreds of miles inland (as in Bangladesh) and elevations up to 4,000 feet. There are great differences from place to place, but we expect that billions of people already have died since the impact. The East Coast of the United States has been devastated for about 30 to 50 miles inland."

11:15 –"NASA here. The Space Station is just now coming into view of the impact site. We will patch the station output to all functioning TV and radio networks and XM radio."

11:17:30 – "My name is commander Clifford Stack, U.S. Navy. I am aboard the Space Station with a crew that is observing and photographing the unbelievable tsunamis that are surging around the world, and we weep for the loss of life. The sun has set over much of the Indian Ocean, but we see a red glow on the horizon.

"We are coming into view, and we are seeing the northern edges of what appears to be an enormous pool of molten lava about 300 kilometers across. Winds appear to be drawn into this furnace, and *a column of smoke and cloud is rising to about 120,000 feet, by rough estimate. The top is being blown to the west over Africa.*

"The eastern edge is obscured by an opaque bed of what looks like steam backlit by the red light. It appears that the Indian Ocean is pouring into the eastern edge and erupting into vast steam explosions.

"You can see what we are seeing in the pictures, but for those on radio, the key point is that the entire area is an enormous boiling mass of smoke and steam, backlit by red light. We can only see the northwest edge, which appears to be on land and swept clear of steam by the radial winds.

"We are moving in on it in darkness with that awful furnace to our west.

"Finally, we regret to report that we are experiencing a micro-gravity caused by a totally unexpected atmospheric drag on the Space Station. We will run the numbers, but it is at least possible that the atmosphere has been expanded in the edges of space, increasing station drag and our eventual descent into the atmosphere. We will confirm when we have done the calculations. Clifford out."

Richard, one of Father John's students, said, "I have KGO radio in San Francisco, which is broadcasting from a helicopter above the city. He reports that both the San Andreas and Hayward faults have ruptured as the pressure waves flexed the earth, and a massive landslide has split the UC Berkeley campus and much of the Oakland hills. So far, no major fires, and the bridges are intact. The San Francisco high-rises appear to have survived pretty well."

The signal from the 50,000-watt station's transmitter, nearly 300 miles distant, was weak but discernable above the crackling background static.

Ken said, "Cathy, monitor XM, I want to hear KGO. Richard, please turn up the volume."

"… *and it appears that emergency services are effective in those areas not totally destroyed by the landslide. The UC Berkeley Memorial Stadium lower side has collapsed, but parts of the eastern stadium appears intact. I am now looking west, and from this vantage point San Francisco appears essentially intact. Massive electrical power outages have occurred, however, and we are reporting from the KGO helicopter above the Oakland Hills as our transmitter near Fremont remains powered by a combination of solar panels and gas generators.*

"I am pivoting around to get a closer look at the Golden Gate Bridge, and something is wrong with the Farallon Islands off the coast of San Francisco. There is massive surf and the islands seem lower. As I watch, a wave now covers the highest peaks, and it is coming this way. It is like the whole ocean is coming at us. We are gaining altitude, as we don't want to be sucked down.

"Water is starting to pour through the Golden Gate Bridge. It is now up to the deck, pouring over the deck, which is being bent inward into the bay – and now it is gone! The approaches still are holding, but the water is still rising. The Farallons are completely under water. That wave must be more than 500 feet high to cover the Farallons.

"It is now pouring over the Presidio and through the Marina district, and still rising. The entire bay is filling up, and still it comes. Lower Berkeley and Oakland are under water, and a wave is moving down toward San Jose. The Bay Bridge is still intact, what I can see of it. The wave is also moving north into San Pablo Bay, sweeping everything below about a 1,000-foot elevation into this

massive pile of floating wreckage. It is like the Japanese tsunami, on steroids.

"*I can't tell you how hard it is to keep talking as I watch in horror millions of lives being lost. I will try my best. "My pilot says that with our airport and essentially the entire Bay Area about to go under water, we are going to try to reach an airport in the Sierra Nevada or even Reno, as we took on extra fuel....*"

KGO went silent. The wall of water had reached the southern portion of the bay, and inundated the transmitter site. Ken blurted, "See if KFBK, 1530, from Sacramento, is still on the air." Richard found the station. Its distant signal was weak, but intelligible. An airborne reporter was flying over Solano County, near Benicia.

"*We are now passing over the Carquinez Strait, where at the moment both road bridges are holding but the lower Amtrak bridge is down. An immense fire is coming from part of the Shell Oil refinery in Martinez, despite the fact that it is mostly under water.*

"*We're following the wave inland, as it heads toward the Sacramento-San Joaquin River Delta. The main portion of the swell is heading roughly for Stockton, but the torrent also is spreading northeasterly, and Sacramento will be next in a very few minutes. As I look southeast in the San Joaquin Valley, all I see is a sheet of water as far as the horizon. No trace of Stockton remains.*

"*We are now approaching Sacramento, and we have caught up with the wave front. It is not as high as when it came in, but as we watch, the Capitol dome is being swallowed by water. The entire west valley to the hills is inundated, but I see a ridge above the water to the west, sort of a peninsula going north.*

"*To the east, the water has reached well into the foothills. I don't know the names of the small towns, but the foothill areas lower than Cameron Park are all drowned. "Far to the north, I am seeing what appears to be an enormous volcanic plume rising. It is probably Mount Shasta.*

"There is also water coming down from the north in a pretty impressive flood. I expect the Oroville dam has failed. The waves are now in contact, but the Oroville flood is simply dwarfed by the wave...."

The station abruptly left the air as its transmitter in Pleasant Grove, 20 miles north of Sacramento, was engulfed.

Father John solemnly said, "I mourn for our friends in Davis. Should we have warned them? Was our fear of ridicule if we had been wrong a factor in thousands of deaths?" No one knew what to reply.

Ken, focusing on the immediate circumstances, said, "David, climb back to your high perch. Can you see in the direction of Shasta? It may be erupting."

In a few minutes, David came back into view. "The trees block the view east, but we have company coming up the road on foot." The words galvanized the entire group, with people running to their trenches and barriers, not knowing what to expect.

David continued, "Two people, a man and a woman, one armed, on foot. They are not trying to hide."

Ken walked to the nearest tree close to the road, and peered around. His neighbors Roger and Linda were walking nervously up the road, each with backpacks on. "Roger," Ken waved a greeting.

Roger and Linda staggered into camp, as people gathered to meet them. "These are my neighbors, Roger and Linda Johnson. Roger works at Adobe and mostly telecommutes from Davis. We talked a bit as I was loading the Jeep, and shared my fears of both being right and being wrong."

Linda said, "Roger did some research after you left, and things were clearly coming apart big time. Websites were down, communications re-directed, chaos. We thought more about what you had said, and then after about an hour decided to try to find you and the mine that you roughly described. When we hit the burned-out store in Salyer, I knew we were close, but we had gone too far. We saw this road, and some signs of recent use. We ran our SUV into some brush and started to walk up.

"We hit Redding just as the president was making his speech. We were still able to buy food with a credit card, and everybody on the road appeared to be hurrying somewhere and didn't care about us."

Ken said, "Glad you are here. That 'locked' gate is actually open. Richard, could you run down with your SUV and help them bring their SUV up here? I really need to hear what we are getting on XM radio."

Cathy chimed in, "While you were listening to AM radio, Janet Napolini came on and said she is now reporting from a safe haven for the government in an enormous underground bunker in a high mountain valley in Shenandoah National Park. The big news items are the massive tsunamis that have swept the coastlines of all oceans, destroying everything at elevations ranging between 1,500 and 2,500 feet. The biggest tsunami of all is moving right now through the Pacific Ocean, and all contact has been lost with Japan and coastal China. There are also tsunami-like waves in all major lakes, seriously damaging all the cities that ring the Great Lakes, for example.

"Second, there are dam failures and earthquakes, including the San Andreas Fault, the Seattle Fault, and the New Madrid Fault, plus volcanic eruptions in widespread locations, including Yellowstone National Park, and elsewhere around the world.

"Third, the enormous smoke and dust cloud has reached north and is starting to cross the equator as it approaches South America. The cloud contains vast amounts of sulfuric acid, and the tops are bright white with an orange tinge.

"There was more, but the sadness and weariness in Janet's voice was palpable. Then the president came on, said briefly that much of the central United States is intact, and we will survive this if we work together and respond intelligently.

"Finally, there was a live report from the International Space Station, which is now slowly spiraling into the atmosphere. It will not survive the week. The astronauts are going to pack all their recordings and data into the Soyuz, and one of them will release it from the station and use its braking motors to go into a higher stable orbit so that all that they have learned will be available sometime in the future."

Ken said, "Sit down everyone. In that excellent report, Cathy, there was one quick phrase that portends doom. The cloud is so bright and full of sulfuric acid that it will drastically cool the Earth. This concept used to be called 'nuclear winter,' but small examples have occurred after massive volcanic eruptions, like Pinatubo in 1991. We are in for a very severe but hopefully short ice age, since the Indian Ocean appears to be pouring into the crater and should eventually cool it.

"We are well placed to get the benefit of the Pacific Ocean, which will be a massive machine to cleanse the air of dust because of the enormous amount of heat stored in its waters. We can expect, however, no help from coastal areas to our west, which are doubtless devastated. This mine must be our hope, our Ark. Fortunately, water is coming out of the mine in that pipe to our west, so there appears to be a spring inside the mine. The water appears OK – at least it is not discolored.

"The key will be warmth and food. The mine will greatly help the former, but there is not nearly enough food to sustain a group this large for perhaps three years.

"We have important choices to make."

4. SCHISM

The SUVs returned in about half an hour.

There was still a lot of chatter on the satellite radio, but it merely seemed to be tallying up the disasters caused by the tsunamis, earthquakes, and volcanic eruptions, including some enormous mega-volcanoes in Yellowstone National Park. All communication with the Southern Hemisphere had ceased, except for Australia, New Zealand, and two research stations on Antarctica. This was worrisome in itself because large parts of South America should have survived the tsunamis. But there was that short report from Bariloche in Argentina about heavy dust and acidic rain falling in a stinging mud.

The sun was setting on that awful day, and sort of by consensus, everybody sat in a circle around the mine entrance. For many minutes, no one spoke. It was clear that the world as they had all known it was gone forever. And if what Ken had predicted comes true, billions more will die just like the dinosaurs – for lack of food.

Sheldon, ever analytical, spoke first. "We must find more food, but the coastal areas are certainly destroyed. There are no real resources inland, and I believe that foraging would be danger-ous because of roving gangs. We have brought a lot of valuable hardware here to the mine, but with the roads likely eradicated not that many miles to our west, that won't help us much. But we need food, and a lot of it."

Linda commented, "I recall that after the Japanese tsunamis, some well-built buildings survived in part. The same thing might be true in Eureka, and in the wreckage we could find canned goods and the like. I don't think we would have to worry about roving gangs."

Another long pause.

Sheldon said, "Perhaps we could send a party to reconnoiter? How many miles is it?"

Ken said, "Well, first, let's get everything stowed and inven-toried in the mine, calculate calorie levels, check the water sup-ply, and determine how many people could survive here for three years. God help us if it is longer than that!"

So in the fading light, work began and went on well into the night, with the Volt's headlights illuminating the cave, because it was the only vehicle small enough to enter the tunnel – with only modest scraping of paint. When darkness had fallen, the group took great care in making sure that no light shone outside the mine.

Sleeping inside the mine was difficult for all of them, but exhaustion was setting in. Meaghan, however, a Newman student, simply sat weeping over loss she could barely imagine.

The guards rotated coverage every four hours as before.

Dawn broke late, because a massive cloud to the east blocked the sun. All night long distant thunder could be heard, and most in the camp attributed it to the eruption of Mt. Shasta.

As the sun cleared the trees, Ken was up above the mine, looking intently at the sky.

He came down as people were cleaning up and preparing breakfast. The scene looked like a student camping trip. No one was smiling, however.

"I hate to always be the bearer of bad news," Ken started, "but so far my pessimism has been justified. We may have less time than we thought. There is a hint of yellow in the sky – most likely the precursor of the sulfuric acid cloud. The fact that it has crossed the equator and penetrated this far north already is very bad news. We will, probably in days, start to lose solar heating, and we will be going all too quickly into a 'nuclear winter' condition. It is going to get cold soon, and next winter will be brutal. Whatever we do, we had better do quickly.

"Anybody have any ideas where we could possibly find food between here and Eureka?"

Linda piped up, "We saw some chickens running around near the burned-out store. Could we get them? And there may be some stuff the looters didn't take."

After some discussion, the group decided that 10 of them, including Ken and Roger, with all five weapons would travel down to the store and see what they could find.

The rest were busy running up an inventory of supplies, and

carefully listing them in a spreadsheet on a laptop. "Careful of your batteries. We soon will be unable to recharge them," said Ken.

"Not for a while," Roger said. "I have a DC-to-AC converter in my SUV, and we all have a lot of 12-volt battery power."

The store was essentially leveled, and some storage sheds had been opened and ransacked, but not burned. In the brush below the store were signs of movement. Chickens! Ken and Roger entered the storehouse and found that a lot of animal feed was strewn all over the floor. Someone was searching for something, but what was left was a holy mess. Still, there was a lot of feed lying around that they could gather to feed the chickens at the mine.

"Roger, run back and bring down the Jeep and SUVs, but stop before you reach the road in case we get company. There is far too much to carry. OK, students, let's find a way to herd the chickens into a confined space."

Ken spotted a six-foot high fence joined by two partially ruined walls, making a three-sided pen, and moving slowly in a large arc, the group slowly forced the chickens up the hill toward the pen. Ken noticed the flock included both hens and roosters – a breeding flock. As they approached the pen, they realized that it contained more chickens than they had realized, perhaps 30 or so.

"Let's catch them one at a time and put them in the storehouse," said Ken. "We can have one person guard them, and the chickens will be in hog heaven with all that feed on the floor."

After much lunging and squawking, the chickens were safely in the storehouse, and only three got away.

Roger came down with the SUV, saw the flock, and said "Not

in my car you don't."

Ken replied, "OK, you can get the feed. I want all that you can scrape up. My Jeep has been through the wars, and not even chickens can make it too bad."

By the afternoon, 27 chickens were herded into a pen they built in a side chamber in the cave, and probably 500 pounds of feed was stacked on the floor. They also found a small number of potatoes, probably seed stock, mixed in the pile on the floor of the storehouse, and these were sorted from the feed and carefully stored.

The inventory was completed, and the conclusions grim. Again, as the sun set, everyone sat in a rough circle.

Ken started, "See that beautiful orange sunset? That is sulfuric acid, and in one day it has become about as bad as Pinatubo was. It is going the get very cold, very soon. Cathy, what have you gotten from the radio?"

"Less and less," she answered. "Only XM is on the air, and the information is dire. The southern United States is already under a dense cloud that is full of dust, and it's settling on everything. The temperature has plummeted. We are getting advisories to stockpile food and fuel and prepare for intense cold."

"Well, they got that right," Ken thought.

"What this means is that we must move promptly if we move at all. Cathy and Linda, what do we have from the inventory?"

Cathy replied, "For a three–year timeline, if we reduce consumption to 1,000 calories per day, our supplies will cover four or five people – no more – assuming we do nothing with the chickens. With their eggs, we could probably keep six people here."

Ken started, "I see three potential courses of action: 1) we all stay here, and hope the cold lasts only one year; 2) split the group, leaving four or five here with all our gear, technology, and chickens, and take the rest on a very dangerous and uncertain quest to find food in what is left of Eureka; or 3) keep the group intact, seal the mine as best we can, and all us of trek to Eureka. Does anyone see any options other than these three? Your thoughts, please? I can think of pros and cons to each argument, and I am sure you can, too. However, I would like to argue against moving inland away from the sea. It is dangerous, and no major town that might have food exists for 100 miles. In any case, it has probably already been plundered."

It took hours to talk it out, with the darkening sky a constant prod. In the end, Sheldon and Veronica would stay, along with Meaghan and two more students, another girl and a Newman boy. They had become attached to the solid security of the mine and the calm, logical presence of Sheldon. They were allowed to keep one handgun, and asked to take care of all the chickens.

Relinquishing all technology as extra weight was amazingly difficult, but they had to travel light with weapons, essential tools, Swiss army knives, clothing, and as much food as they could carry. Ken split the seed stock in two, taking cool-season vegetables should things get better, and leaving the rest in the mine. They raided a small solar cell from one SUV, with a laptop, 12-volt light, and a hand-held digital calculator. Ken kept his Canon EOS camera and lenses, a good set of binoculars, and a few CDs and DVDs because they could play on the laptop.

The next morning, Ken, Cathy, Roger, Linda, David, Father John, and nine students crammed into two SUVs, determined to drive as far as they could.

The Volt, Jeep, and another SUV were left at the mine, with the Volt almost blocking the mine entrance all by itself. To everyone's amazement, the 110-volt electricity was still on.

Farewells were brief but moving. The drive down the gloomy road was matched by the uncertainties of this leap into nothingness. They agreed that they would not return if they did not find food, because the supplies in the mine would not be sufficient for the entire group. They reset the gate, and this time did a better job securing the lock.

They went on, with Ken, Roger, and David walking spread out across the road, guns at the ready position.

In a few miles, they were approaching Willow Creek junction. All the dwellings on the south and west side of the road were burned, but those north and east seemed untouched. As they slowly walked into town, they heard a loud shot from somewhere up in the hills northeast of the town, at some distance.

Ken triggered a single shot into the air, and waited. Nothing. No further shots were forthcoming, as they moved slowly into the town and reached the junction leading to Arcata, now 40 miles west. They carefully brought up the SUVs, one at a time, and they turned toward the coast.

They had gone only a few miles, dropping down into Redwood Creek, when devastation met their eyes. The entire valley below them had been swept clear of trees, dwellings, everything. A windrow of logs blocked the road, and they realized they would have to abandon the SUVs. Ken and Roger drove them well off the road into brush, covered them, and everyone carried all they could on their backs.

The going was actually easy descending into the valley because the road was still intact and all tree trunks had been swept away – probably as the tsunami retreated. Only the abutments of the bridge remained, but because the stream was shallow, they were able to cross it. They climbed back up the ridge, re-entering an intact forest above the reach of the tsunami, and stopped near the road as the sun was setting. It was already cold, but they did not dare build a fire. As they examined their packs, with no more than four or five days' supply of food, the reality and uncertainties of their decision hung in the air like a specter. Sleep was not easy, and they rotated at standing guard; however, no one had seen or heard any activity. The woods were bathed in an eerie silence. The physical gloom and the pervasive sense of melancholy and foreboding reinforced and fed on each other. No one knew what the morning would hold.

The next morning, dawn illuminated a gray sky. The sun was still visible, but dim, and the gray haze extended as far up as anyone could see. The air seemed gritty.

Gathering up their packs, they almost ran out of the woods, knowing that they could not bear the suspense. Finally, they reached the ridge top, and saw the plain below.

Ken brought out his binoculars, as they all sat in silent awe of the devastation. The plain had been swept clean. There was no trace whatsoever of Arcata, now just a few miles away. The retreating tsunami had swept the plain clean of debris, except for occasional clumps where some obstruction had persisted. Humboldt Bay itself looked different from Ken's recollection, with a very large gap into the ocean, almost eliminating the long peninsula that used to exist.

Looking closely where Eureka should have been, Ken saw

more numerous debris piles that had not been swept out to sea. It is there, in the wreckage of the city, where they might find food and shelter. A desperate hope, but little else remained.

They hurried down the road, clear of debris but with culverts and bridges swept away. Still, the road was the best place for walking. When the group reached Mad River, all they saw was an occasional Redwood trunk jammed against some culvert. They hiked toward the ocean. The cold wind was biting now, even though it was May.

The laceration of the plain was more complex than what they had seen from the ridge. The outrushing water had scoured channels, and the Mad River was starting to cut a new channel in the sandy debris. Pools of water were trapped in depressions, and some of the ground that looked solid turned out to be almost like quicksand, so walking on the remains of the road was still the best route for the group.

The U.S. 101 freeway bridge across the Mad River had been destroyed, but the spans lay in the river in such a way that the group could cross if they were very cautious. They helped each other leap from one toppled piling to the next, and hurried on as best they could toward the remains of Eureka. They saw no trace of dwellings, houses, cars or, thankfully, bodies. It looked like a large sandy beach. And to make the scene complete, thousands of seagulls were scavenging the abundant fish and other detritus that remained in pools behind obstructions. The birds lent a cheery air to an otherwise grim scene.

As the group arrived at what they presumed was Eureka, it was clear that the area had been vastly modified by the tsunami. A bay that had been connected to the ocean by a narrow channel was now obliterated, and had become part of a long expanse of ocean. Large waves were rolling in and breaking on the edge of debris that probably was the remains of bayside roads and buildings. Considerable erosion was occurring in the ubiquitous sandy layer that covered everything to a depth of a foot or more.

One pile of debris was especially extensive. Walking up to and around it, the group suddenly came to pavement that was painted "Emergency Vehicles Only."

"It was a hospital," Roger said. "They are often more substantial to meet California earthquake codes."

At the southeast corner, an enormous pile of wood that had been caught by the building – boards and tree trunks, mostly – was all jammed in with sand and dirt. But one wall could be seen rising about 12 feet above ground level.

"See if there is a way in," urged Ken. It was a real mess, and reminded Ken of what the wreckage of the World Trade Center in New York looked like as people sifted through the wreckage to try to find victims in the first days.

"I found an intact window," yelled Alice, one of Ken's student workers. She was a slight figure and had crawled into a pile to be rewarded by an intact window on the south side of the hospital.

"It would have been parallel to the tsunami," said Ken. "Careful, and see if we can get in without breaking it too badly."

No such luck. It was not designed to open, so three of Ken's workers carefully chipped away at the edges until it came free.

Ken was carrying one of the three wind-up flashlights, and crawled into the gap. He shone the light into the space, and was rewarded by a storeroom, essentially intact, with no sand or mud inside.

Two students used saws to make the access easier, and Ken slid through the window and dropped to the floor about six feet below. The floor was dry. "Come on in," he relayed back to the group. In about 15 minutes, all 15 members were down and in, and they separated into teams to explore what was left of the building.

The room seemed to be a storeroom for the hospital – not very urgent stuff but needed in large numbers. Vast piles of laundered hospital gowns filled shelves, black plastic trash bags in some numbers, soap, toilet paper, paper towels, and other supplies. Another wall was essentially all bedpans. One wall had pull-out boxed shelves with catheters, and other hardware. A tub of things called "sharps" with a red label was waiting for recycling or something. "Not a great start," thought Ken. Opening the door, he found some sand, and just about 30 feet west, the ceiling had collapsed into the floor. No passage was possible.

A corridor led east for about 30 feet before turning right. Ken found two more rooms, and a hall that went north until it, too, was blocked by debris. Again the floor was covered with dirt and sand. But at the very end, he spotted a larger room with light showing through a gap between the fallen ceiling and the east wall. The gap was not very large but could be useful as a chimney. "Finally something of some use," said Ken. In one of the side rooms was a large sealed set of powdered milk and pre-mixed infant formulas. There must have been hundreds of pounds of the stuff, all in sealed canisters. The other room had mostly parts for repairing beds and the like, regretfully without the tools to fix them. Chairs, desks, and tables, all with some sort of damage, were awaiting repair.

Ken's group discovered one more corridor at the north end of the collapsed hall, leading west. It, too, had been crushed. A set of stairs led down to another area, but halfway down, the place was full of sand, and no further progress was possible.

Ken asked the group to gather in the farthest north room, which was full of spare furniture, probably repaired. He said, "I propose that we use this room as our main working room. We could have a fire here if we did some building on that gap to make it a chimney. Right next door is the powdered milk, and let's not use that room because we want to preserve it. It also has very little floor space. The corner room looks like a good sleeping area, but it has no windows. Let's find as much wire as we can and place the solar panel up in the debris, but hidden, and run the wire down to the light bulb. Thus, we would have some light while the sun shines.

"We need to organize our teams, because we still should maintain a night watch. We also can rotate duties necessary to make this refuge livable. I propose that the married pairs each form a team, and then Father John and senior students lead a third group. David and Alice, you both have shown real initiative. I would propose that you be interim joint student heads of Team 3. We will find better names later that you can choose for yourselves.

"Sleep on it, then I propose that we have a drawing tomorrow morning for people who choose to be in one team or the other. Let's try to align people with their friends, because we are going to have to become one enormous family to survive.

"Once that is done, we should decide which duties need to be distributed. The most urgent is our search for food, and I propose two of the teams work on that tomorrow, while the third team stays here and builds a heating system, identifies how we handle human waste, obtains storage for our limited food supply – unless you are anxious to live on powdered milk indefinitely – and identify a nearby source of drinkable water."

Not much could be done that evening, but the next morning, the refugees gathered in a large circle. By accident, men and women were almost equal in number. The Newman group was mostly female, and Ken's students were two-thirds men. They wrote first and second choices on each slip of paper, and placed them into a large bowl.

Not surprisingly, the Newman students mostly went with Father John – who insisted from now on to be called John – and the physics students favored Ken. Roger had an obviously affectionate pair. They transferred one extra woman to Roger's team, and one guy to John's, and the teams were set.

In the days that followed, the groups reconfigured the entire space and set up a dormitory, solar-powered lights, and a cooking area. They brought in a great quantity of wood, and built a Franklin stove-like contraption from any metals they could find, including some intact hospital heating and cooling ductwork.

The result was a fire cone in the middle of the room on a raised brick platform, and ducting that took the smoke across the room to the crack in the ceiling, now remade into a chimney. The cheery fire was warming and the light it cast was important, and every day the group filled the corridors with any wood of the right size they could find.

The sky remained ashen gray, but the visibility was not too bad. Still, the sun seemed so weak and gave little heat. The air was getting colder, and it was only the beginning of June. Ken and his students designed a meteorology protocol, with measurements twice a day – dawn and 4:00 p.m. – using their only thermometer, a little one hanging from the zipper of an REI jacket.

The teams systematically surveyed all other debris piles. Down by the ocean, the waves were uncovering items that the retreating tsunami had washed to the shore. In one pile they found items likely from a destroyed hardware store, including hammers and saws, and even a sledgehammer – all too heavy to have floated away on the back flood.

Finally, six days later, success. Roger's team found a pile that was clearly from a major supermarket, now swept totally clean except for one corner in which a large freezer had survived the flood. Working together, all three teams managed to dig the door free of the sand, and inside was a treasure: tons of meat, either still frozen or very cold, preserved by the sand and debris that covered it.

They closed the door to keep the food cold, and the teams made immediate plans to cook or smoke as much of the meat as possible before it thawed and was ruined. The cool weather conditions were helping to preserve the meat long enough to prepare it for later consumption.

In addition, by scraping, the teams unearthed cans just below the surface of the sand in a debris pile stretching toward the sea. Although many of the cans lacked labels, they collected all of them.

Ever innovative, Alice concocted a plan to preserve the meat. "I propose we sterilize that large broken refrigerator that we were trying to remove from the junk room. We would heat it with a pile of hot coals before putting in the food. We could use bedpans, sealed with aluminum foil, while the coals are still hot, and then we could put them inside the refrigerator. With the doors closed, and by maintaining strict hygiene, the meat could last a long time. We could move it into Room 3 with all the dried milk powder."

"Good idea," said Ken. "But let's not forget the large mass of frozen meat in the locker, and the fact that it is very cold. By fall, it might stay frozen all by itself, sort of the way they stored their fall moose in Alaska. We should open the door only for the shortest possible period of time, and bring out enough meat to fill Alice's refrigerator, then immediately close the door."

Obtaining water proved more difficult. Numerous small streams were flowing in the area, but the water was salty. About a mile inland and up a small hill, a stream flowed down from a ridge. It had a slightly salty taste, but it was the best water source they could find. The teams diverted the stream into a channel to bring it near the hospital wreckage, a task made easier because all they had to do was scribe a small furrow in the sand and the stream did all the rest.

They constructed a small pool against the eastern outside wall of the hospital so that the water ran down the south side of the building toward the sea, and they built a small bridge to allow access to the door. At the far end, well down and away from the entrance, John's team built latrines so the stream could carry away the waste.

A sense of relief swept through the refugees, and they made plans to travel back to Salyer to tell the mine group what they had found. The entire group needed to organize and prepare for a year without a summer.

5. THE COLD: YEAR 1

Two weeks had passed, and the official start of summer was approaching. Alice's group thawed and roasted many pounds of turkey, steak, pork, and chicken, and crammed it into bedpans that nearly filled the old broken refrigerator.

Ken had the idea of cooling the refrigerator by conduction – the most efficient way to move heat. He found some crumpled aluminum awning structure in the sand in front of the hospital mound, built a 10-foot long section in a rough beam, and hooked an old aluminum radiator grill on one end. He laboriously drilled a hole in the concrete wall, and thrust the aluminum pipe through it. The old radiator was on the outside of the wall in the shade of a debris pile and the east wall of the hospital, but fully exposed to outside air. He then wrapped a portion of the wall in a thick layer of hospital gowns, and fanned the aluminum into a large flat array, which passed through the edge of the partially open door. The whole array was covered with hospital gowns that also sealed the gaps in the door.

Within a few hours, the thermometer showed that the inside temperature had been lowered to 36 degrees F, nearly as cold as the outdoor temperature, which was approaching freezing each night.

The entire group was trying desperately to keep up their spirits. All three teams agreed that they wanted a window in the dormitory, Room 2, after discovering a series of parts for replacing broken windows in the junk rooms, which by now had been largely emptied of junk. They managed to pound a rectangular hole through the south wall of the hospital, but reinforcing bars prevented them from squaring the opening, and their attempt to cut through the bars dulled the blade of their only metal saw, almost to the point of uselessness. With perseverance, they succeeded in making the hole, and installed three panes of glass for insulation, jamming the windows in with shims, and using mud as an air sealant.

In addition, they were able to repair the existing window and installed triple-pane glass, so that two of the four rooms now had outside light, and the fourth room had a fireplace.

Every morning, Ken and his students took meteorological readings, and John said Mass in the first room, which had an outside door. He set up a small altar, and offered communion to those who so wished. The amount of bread was minuscule, barely visible to the eye, as one host had to handle the whole congregation. Ken and Cathy usually attended Mass, as did most of the Newman students, but many of Ken's physics students stayed away. One refrain that Ken often heard was, "How could a good God allow this to happen to billions of people?"

After breakfast the work details were spread out, often with all three teams out searching for food or anything useful.

Each afternoon before dinner, Ken and his students took meteorological readings. When the external exploring parties had come in, the teams held a group meeting.

After dinner, the group engaged in some light entertainment that included skits, songs, games – especially card games from a single packet that someone had brought – and books recited from memory as best they could. They had the one laptop computer, and were able to recharge its battery with the solar panel. Every night, they played a CD on the laptop for music from a small collection that Ken had in his Volt. Once a week on the laptop, they played one of the seven video DVDs that Ken had put in his backpack, but only one group at a time was allowed to watch because the screen was so small. Thus, it would take 21 weeks to cycle all the groups through all of the DVDs.

At 10:00 p.m. everyone went to bed. The dormitory was arranged by teams, and all of the refugees agreed upon a strict prohibition against any sex that might result in pregnancy, because birth of a baby under such conditions would be very difficult. In fact, most social interactions were more brother- or sister-like.

Ken and his meteorological team prepared to deliver a briefing on July 1.

"Our troubles are not through, despite all the progress we have made," began Ken. "First, and most ominous, nothing much is happening. What I mean is that you have all noticed that the wind has dropped to zero, except for a nightly local downslope wind, and the ocean has become dead calm. I wish Sheldon were here, but I believe this says that the normal cycling of solar heat from the equator toward the pole that causes the winds has ceased. The equator is now reflecting so much light back into space that the equatorial heat engine is failing.

"Nevertheless, an enormous amount of heat is stored in the oceans, and I expect incredibly strong storms are occurring with the warm ocean, which is the best way to clear the atmosphere. I have no idea how long it will take, but the process is very efficient. It does not, however, affect the stratospheric sulfuric acid layer that is giving us our deep orange sunsets. Our meteorological team is trying to quantify this color, because when it starts to fade we will be coming out of the woods.

"However, you also notice that the sky, though hazy, is still pretty clear. The massive clouds and dust referred to by the International Space Station have not reached this far north. Thus, the North Pole continues to bleed heat into space without being supplied with new heat from the equator. I fear that we are going to build up a so-called 'Siberian high' that will move very cold air south into our area, and not too far in the future. Despite the higher sun and longer days, the temperature continues to drop, and goes below freezing every night.

"We are going to have to prepare for really intense cold and a longer winter. Let's assume it is so cold outside that we can't leave these rooms. What are the consequences?"

A general discussion ensued, in which almost everybody contributed. They discussed and solved problems, including inadequacy of heat, which they decided to remedy by using additional fuel inside, and disposal of bodily waste by using the sand in the basement as an inside latrine. They would dig and extend trenches as far from the building as possible, and use wood ashes daily to cover them.

They decided to move a lot of the frozen food from the locker to just outside the door and cover it with hospital gowns to keep it frozen. They would immediately intensify their search for canned food because if the cans froze, they might be ruined.

The group decided to improve their water supply by digging a new, deep pond just west of the entry bridge. They resolved to drill through the hospital wall and install a pipe that would lead from the pond to a holding tank, as large as would fit inside Room 1.

The fears seemed to fade a bit as each day was essentially a copy of the one before. Even the temperature seemed to have stabilized. But the ocean was flat as a millpond, totally without waves. The silence was eerie. But the good news was that excellent scavenging was occurring in the newly exposed debris field at the edge of the ocean. Lack of waves made access easy, even into shallow waters. Clearly, a lot of stuff had been dumped into what had been a bay, then covered up with sand. The ocean had now exposed it, including a second small cache of food cans from some unknown upslope market.

July 4 broke clear as a bell. The sky was blue, the sun was high in the sky and warm. Everyone came out and reveled in the morning of hope. They made plans for a trip up to the mine site, buoyed by the newly discovered food caches on the beach. Team 3, minus John, would make the trip, carrying two of the three remaining guns, and a few knives in case they encountered trouble.

The wind, however, was picking up from the northeast. It had a chill to it. By noon, the temperature, which had been rising, started to drop as the wind picked up. Ken and his meteorological team huddled in the lee of the building. They were loath to be the bearers of bad news when everyone else was so exuberant. But by 3:00 p.m., they had no choice but to report their findings. The wind was now bitterly cold, and the temperature went below freezing well before sunset. People were coming indoors on their own, clutching their miserably inadequate hospital gowns, used as outer garments.

At the afternoon briefing, Ken was blunt: "We are now in for a very cold period. I propose we initiate the measures we have planned and hope that the freeze does not last long. Because of the strengthened sun, I am moving the solar panel to a more exposed location to get more power. We have all the water we can store, but I want a path cleared to better access the eastern pond if we have to chip ice from it."

Ginger, one of John's team members, started to quietly sob. Others comforted her, but gloom filled the room.

Because of the depressing situation, the teams decided to prepare a better dinner than usual. They had found a can of cranberry sauce, and broke out and warmed the turkey, and had canned peaches for dessert.

The next morning dawned very cold, and the increasing winds created a modest dust storm from the north to northeast. The morning temperature reading was 18 degrees below zero F – close to the low end of the scale on the mini thermometer. Ken and the meteorological team huddled and tried to work out a protocol that would handle even colder temperatures. They devised several plans, including the temperature drop at a fixed time of exposure to a temperature gradient along a steel pipe with one end in water and the other outside.

During the day, a battle ensued between the warm sun and the bitter wind. In sheltered alcoves on the south wall of the hospital, the temperature at noon was pleasant. But as the sun set lower in the sky, the cold set in.

Any thought of Team 3 trying to reach the mine was now out of the question. The group realized that it was probably even colder up there, with altitude and distance from the ocean. Even scavenging at noon was a trial, and teams all went out together so that they could protect each other if a twisted ankle or other accident would make return to the hospital difficult.

The dormitory was getting colder, so they re-arranged beds in the main room. They also moved some of the canned goods that were subject to freezing into the room, which suddenly became more crowded; however, with the eternal fire, at least it was warm.

In one meeting, Ken mentioned that the fire would be extremely hard to reignite if it ever went out. The group members had very few matches among them, and they were only the paper kind that were iffy for ignition. The group decided to build a second fireplace near the entrance in Room 1, and the task galvanized everyone for weeks. They modified the door with an immovable section at the top, and the smokestack ran through it and up about 10 feet into the air. The top of the stack, probably 15 feet above ground, had a re-entrant cover to protect it against water or snow.

By now the group had found several tubes and pipes, and these led to a fire cone-like device above a fire that was set in bricks at about chest height. That way, even if the reservoir spilled, the fire would not be extinguished.

Teams were given the task of maintaining the second fire, which, because of its configuration, needed smaller pieces of wood. With several wood saws rescued from the bay, a regular rotation was set for the teams to go out, find wood, and bring in pieces before the cold got to them.

An unexpected benefit to the second fire was that its heat actually drifted up the corridor toward the main room and fire, because it was pulled by the larger volume of hot air up the chimney of the main fire. Also, the light was welcome, especially as the summer-that-didn't-happen turned into fall.

Temperatures began to decline again, now dropping to very cold levels at night, estimated at 80 to 90 degrees below zero F. Even in the daytime, the temperature never got much higher than 15 degrees F. The ground outside was frozen solid, and the creek ceased to flow. Now a major task was to break up ice from the ponds to put into a large kettle next to the fire to furnish drinking water and a tiny amount of warm water every few days for bathing.

About that time, the ocean near the shore froze over, probably enhanced by the total lack of wave motion. The sharp cracking and popping sounds they began hearing in the distance probably were not gunshots, but more likely came from trees as they froze and shattered.

"The redwoods will never survive this cold," said Ken. Jeanette, one of his senior physics students, chimed in, "Well, these may help." In her hand were four small redwood burls in a package designed for tourist sales. She had picked them up at the Salyer store and kept them warm.

"You have an idea, I'm sure, how important that may be in the future," said Ken. He almost added "… if this cold ever lets up," but caught himself in time. He was aware that the Earth in the past had gone through a "snowball" phase when it was almost entirely coated with glaciers.

By December, the dark and cold were now intense, although the stars shone brightly. On occasion, northern lights were visible on the northern horizon, but breathing was very difficult, and face masks of greater and greater complexity were needed to go outside. Finally, a full-face mask was required for breathing through a tube that ran down inside the outer clothing so that the air would be warmed before it reached the nose or mouth. The temperature by now was just an estimate, but could be as low as 120 below zero F.

The group took extra care in trying to make Christmas special. John had a special Mass with lots of singing, and almost everybody, even agnostics, chimed in. Weeks of preparation and training paid off, and it was beautiful.

There were no presents, but each person was figuratively "given" (in secret) a virtual gift that would be claimed once the cold relented. Alice and Jeanette thawed and heated four entire turkeys, and with the last of the cranberry sauce and some macaroni and cheese found sealed in a tin, dinner was very special. Everyone was warm and had a full stomach.

As various ideas for entertainment became stale, John proposed a new phase in which everyone had to write a book in their head, and deliver it chapter by chapter. Three people were to work together, and the books would be read in rotating sequence to allow time to mentally compose the next chapter. In the beginning, no one wanted to go first, so Ken volunteered. Ken's story was an ecological fantasy about two planets that shared information on the greenhouse effect. Alice was next, and to everyone's surprise, the normally reticent Linda volunteered to tell her story. Alice had a romantic fantasy involving telepathy. Linda's was a complex spy story.

Each was to finish his or her story in a month.

By February, the cold was brutal. Temperatures now reached an estimated 130 degrees below zero F at night, and rose to perhaps 65 below zero F during the day. But the sky was clear, and the days became longer. The orange color in the sunsets was distinctly weaker than before.

It was early March when a large cloud was seen on the southern horizon, and the steady northeast winds of the past nine months weakened and died. A massive snowstorm struck the coast two days later, but temperatures rose sharply into the 20s. It seemed like a heat spell. Snow continued falling for almost a month, with short breaks of intense cold. Luckily, these periods of northeast winds were strong, and blew some of the snow away before the next batch arrived. The hospital refuge was largely buried, so extensions had to be added to both chimneys to avoid being covered up.

On April 3, everyone awoke to a strange rumble. Going outside, they climbed the drifts and saw to the west the ocean surf breaking on the ice shelf. It was still miles out to sea, but hope was suddenly a reality. There would be a spring after all. More snow followed, just to dampen their enthusiasm.

About one month later, the first rains arrived. Initially, it made a slushy mess of the snow, which still was almost 20 feet deep on the average, but gradually the rain melted the snow. Going outside was now almost impossible, and water started to leak into their refuge from several directions. Plugging and bailing became the task of the day, while the group desperately tried to keep the four main rooms dry.

But by May, bare ground was staring to show and their creek started to flow again, but at perhaps 10 times the previous flow. The thaw exposed sandy areas where they could walk, and every day the dry areas expanded. The temperature never rose much higher than 45 degrees F, but it was enough. The bulky outer clothing from the ever-abundant hospital gowns were thankfully shed, and people were able to wash their clothes for the first time in months. Soon the area south of the refuge was festooned with clothes drying on salvaged telephone wires. Most nights now stayed above freezing.

June arrived, and the plain near the ocean was now essentially free of snow. The hills and mountains to the east, however, were still clothed in heavy blankets of snow. Travel was limited, and roaring streams were pouring down onto the plain from every height. These were essentially impossible to cross. Most of the ground was still frozen when probed six inches deep, and the surface was saturated with water.

About this time, the massive flow of the Mad River was driving enormous slabs of ice out of the bay and into the ocean. The surf arrived close to the prior beach line, but the sea was about eight feet lower in elevation than before.

By late June, the temperatures had stabilized with the nights barely above freezing because of the cold winds that came down from the snowpack in the hills. Daytime temperatures would occasionally reach 50 degrees F, or so. The saturated ground was starting to dry, but deep down it was still frozen.

Everyone had a bad case of what used to be known in Alaska as "cabin fever" as the result of being cooped up for months at a time during long Alaska winters. All three teams set out to make a sort of classroom outside in a protected south-facing alcove in the hospital debris pile, so that the afternoon briefings were now outdoors. The old dormitory was re-established, and the secondary fire was extinguished after Ken's team had mastered the art of starting a fire without matches. Old skills were once again vital.

On June 21, the official first day of summer, the normal tasks were canceled for an all-day briefing and planning session.

Ken started the meeting, and then Roger's team and John's team would follow, each with their own focus. Ken's team was the environment team, but people were being traded around based on their skills.

Ken began, "I think we were saved by the fact that much of the Toutatis impact crater was in the Indian Ocean. Clearly, the ocean rushed in and cooled the surface lava lake, generating massive clouds of steam that covered the middle latitudes of the Earth but also efficiently took out the impact dust cloud. Thus, the 'nuclear winter' was brutal, but short. We still have the high stratospheric sulfate levels. It will take a few years to clear, based on the Pinatubo experience, but as it dies there will be additional warming.

"The drop in the sea level indicates the presence of a lot of ice in the northern latitudes. I expect there has been a massive growth in snow pack and eventually glaciers. We are probably in a mini ice age right now. We still have, I expect, a lot of excess CO_2 in the atmosphere, which will aid in heating us up, eventually. A last little gift from our fossil fuel debauch.

"So we must assume that the climate we have in this ocean-moderated plain will be the new norm, with local weather probably like Homer, Alaska, used to have. That is important because we are eventually going to have to raise our own food in these conditions. We are already seeing temperatures in the old freezer starting to rise, and we should probably have another of Alice's 'cook and preserve' sessions soon. We are still finding canned goods, but most are now ruined and the cans split because of being frozen solid.

"Finally, along those lines, I haven't found even a trace of green anywhere. Not a blade of grass. I want to get back into the edge of the forest once the snow melts back, but I expect all the trees that adapted to the old Eureka climate are dead because of the intense cold and the deeply frozen ground.

"But we have some seeds, a few seed potatoes, and some of them could be made to grow if we build a sort of greenhouse, and use wood fires to heat it. I propose that is one of our next efforts. Thanks to Jeanette's foresight, we actually have some redwood burls. I propose we try to sprout half of them in our greenhouse. We have seeds for cool-season crops – snow peas, chard, and potatoes. We should get them into the ground soon, and meanwhile mine the sub-basement for human waste – I know, the 'ugh' factor – and start to develop a fertilizer compost heap out here. I would like to propose that Cathy and Linda lead the garden team.

"However, in summary, we have to assume the worst. The tsunami eradicated all civilization near the oceans, leaving only inland sites relatively safe. The intense cold that followed devastated all inland regions and covered them with snow and ice. Survival is going to be at best spotty. Islands of people who prepared were lucky, but their ability to dig themselves out of a new Arctic environment will determine their survivability."

Roger took over for the technology team that, in fact, used a lot of Ken's people.

"We carried down from the cave precious little technology. A solar panel, two hand-held calculators, one laptop, a good digital camera, and a good pair of binoculars, but not much more. The wrecked hospital has some resources, fluorescent light bulbs and fixtures, in good number, some wire, and a few other things.

"Through scavenging, we are constantly finding hardware in the mud of the harbor. Chief among these was a generator probably designed to go onto a small windmill, but wrapped in shrink-wrap and clear of debris. We have yet to find a voltmeter that works.

"Our first effort must be power, and we have a plan. About a quarter mile south of here, a stream flows over a roadway. The far edge of the road drops about 15 feet into a trench cut by the stream when it was more vigorous earlier this spring. We have several long steel rods, and a pipe that slides over one. I propose we make a waterwheel, hook up the generator, and run power lines to the hospital.

"Finally, I suggest that we make every effort to get back to the mine, rescue the people there, and bring down here as much technology as we can carry."

After a brief pause, Roger continued, "We now have a plan to get to the mine site. We are building snowshoes from waste lumber, and three sleds capable of carrying food on the way up, and hardware on the way down. We have five extra sets of snowshoes for the mine team. We even have a cage on a sled that could hold chickens.

"The problem has been the Mad River. In flood, there was no way we could cross it. But is has receded a bit, and we have now designed a suspension bridge to let us get to one of the surviving freeway spans in the river. We are going to need a lot of labor to pull this off.

"What I desire most is getting radios down here and initiating a search for other groups that may have survived."

After some discussion, the group decided that a small contingent, including Cathy and Linda, should stay at the hospital with one weapon, but most would translocate to the Mad River Bridge. The presence of essentially unlimited labor soon had the shaky bridge stabilized with wires out to the remaining span that was above water.

The group made several trips across the bridge until all supplies and sleds were on the far side.

The next day, they began to hike back on the highway and up to the snow line, dragging the sleds across the sand. The snow line was at almost 2,000 feet, covering just the top of the first ridge. They made a camp just below the snow, and the next day they crossed the snow and headed down the ridge toward Redwood Creek. Here the snow was deeper and heavily crusted from the rain that fell on it, so walking was easy and the sleds pulled more smoothly.

Several snow bridges spanned the creek, and after considerable exploration and care, the group made a crossing. It was difficult, but the team hauled all of the equipment up the grade to the ridge near the town and road junction of Willow Creek. They found no tracks in the snow, human or animal. But the surface was hard, so if tracks were made after the rain, they might not show. They made the last camp at Willow Creek using a still-intact building for shelter, and two people would stay behind with two guns to protect the food.

A group of the most vigorous students with John, Ken, and Roger headed out on the next day. The trees were standing, but the needles were brown and brittle.

Soon they found trees that at least looked like the ones near the mine access road gate, with a gap between them that might have held a road. They estimated that the snow was about 15 feet deep at that point. Up the hill they struggled, dragging the sleds. As they gained elevation and moved out of the heavy tree cover, the snow became softer, as though it had never melted, and strong winds had swept away all snow from a few exposed rock faces. One loomed above them, similar to the one above the mine, but no sign of the mine entrance appeared.

Probing with poles, they found what appeared to be a vehicle under about five or six feet of snow. They finally found the edge of the mine entrance, and began digging with the extra snowshoes. A sense of foreboding descended on the team. Something had gone terribly wrong at the mine.

Suddenly there was a hollow in the entrance, and they had broken through to the west edge of the tunnel. Snow was much thinner now, and to their surprise they spotted one of the SUVs, a Ford Explorer, jammed into the entrance, not the Volt they had expected.

Brushing snow from the driver's side window, they could dimly see bodies. The flashlight revealed a bizarre scene. All five of the mine team members were leaning back in their seats, looking in all regards to be asleep. They forced the door open, and the truth was revealed. All five were frozen solid, perfectly preserved, but very dead. No sign of trauma appeared on their faces – they had endured what appeared to be a peaceful death.

The team cleared the tunnel to the SUV, removed the bodies and laid them in shallow trenches in the snow so they wouldn't thaw prematurely. Squeezing between the SUV and the tunnel entrance, they found the mine tunnel in exceptionally good order. Shelves were still stacked with food cans, largely unopened. Shelves that the mine team had made held all the equipment that had not gone down to the ocean, including a pistol, two radios, some tools, and a logbook with careful entries. A Garmin GPS unit was on a shelf, and when triggered on, it still worked. Walking back farther, Ken saw something moving. It was a chicken.

It was not easy, but eventually they found and captured 16 chickens – some appearing to be young, all skinny, and none in good shape. Some feed that the chickens couldn't reach remained. Bunches of bones hinted at cannibalism.

The frozen ground made burial of the dead impossible, and hauling them back to the hospital would take a lot of effort. The sleds were needed for the tools, logs, and chickens and as much food as they would be able to load. Ken recovered the seed stocks, which had been split up. They brought the bodies back into the mine and laid them out carefully in a deep tunnel. They used rocks to cover them, and from his breviary, Father John conducted a small funeral service. "Sheldon saved our lives," Ken added. "If he had not alerted us, it would have been too late to save any of us."

Ken flipped through the logbook, which contained a lot of information. The latter entries revealed that the cave group members were in the habit of all getting into the Volt and using the battery to play a DVD or a CD. About once a week, they would start the engine for a while to recharge the battery. The last entry mentioned that because of the cold, they would switch to using the Explorer.

"Carbon monoxide poisoning, I expect," said Ken. "In cold conditions, the catalytic converter does not become effective until it is warm, and because warm exhaust rises, I bet they were overcome and fell asleep, never to re-awaken. Not a bad way to go, I guess." He turned so as to hide the tears he was shedding over the loss of his dear friend Sheldon, who had saved all their lives.

The trip back was much easier, because the team had a trail to follow. At Willow Creek, they joined the rest of the team members, who had searched the standing buildings but found little of interest except a small tool kit. On the way back, they were generally losing elevation and the going was easier.

As they went below the snow line, they were able to carry most of the stuff on their backs – everything except the chicken cage, the remaining chicken food, and a few pieces of heavy hardware from Ken's Jeep.

At the edge of the Mad River Bridge, they set down about half of the heavy supplies. They were able to achieve the tricky crossing of the Mad River, and they trekked the rest of the 10 miles to the hospital refuge.

Six days after they had departed, the group arrived back at the hospital to an enthusiastic welcome, tempered by the obvious absence of the five mine team members. They were physically and mentally exhausted, and collapsed into bed without even unloading the sleds and packs. Only the chickens were released into a makeshift pen in Room 1, until a better pen could be built. The presence of the chickens was more than welcome because they were the only form of life that the refugees in Eureka had seen in more than a year.

The next day, half the membership took to unloading the treasures from the mine, and the other half went back to the Mad River Bridge to collect what was there.

Roger immediately gathered all the technological equipment so laboriously dragged down and carried, especially the AC-to-DC converter and the quick-start battery charger from Ken's Jeep, which had a DC-to-AC inverter, and an AM-FM radio. He also collected the Garmin GPS, which still worked because the satellites were pretty self-sufficient and in an orbit higher than the drag field that probably by now had brought down the International Space Station.

Cathy and Linda carefully triaged the new seed stock, and showed the mine rescue team the start of a greenhouse in an alcove against a low hospital wall, near the southwest corner of the debris mound.

John's group "adopted" the chickens and began building an outside pen to supplement the inside pen, which was to be used only for roosting.

While they didn't have a lot of food, it was of high quality, including a few pounds of flour, yeast, and some sugar. John pleaded for and was given five pounds of the flour so he could make hosts for communion. By now, his intelligent and rational spirituality had won over most skeptics to some degree, and three in the group had asked to become Catholic.

When Ken was in the cave, he had stuffed three books into his backpack and carried them down to the hospital. They were Father John's *Bible*, the *Handbook of Chemistry and Physics*, and an old *American Institute of Physics Handbook*. One set of his CDs contained the *Encyclopaedia Britannica*.

They spent almost all daylight hours sorting and storing their newly gained supplies, but plans for the next day were to read Veronica's log.

6. VERONICA'S LOG

After breakfast everyone gathered in the south shelter near the bridge, where benches had been set up to make it the best place for an outdoor briefing. They asked Father John to read Veronica's log.

May 23 – Housekeeping. Eureka team has left. All of us know what a chance they are taking. We really could have kept more here in the mine, especially with the chickens, but not everybody. So it is probably best to send the strongest possible team to face the unknown.

Radio. The emergency broadcast system appears up and broadcasting, and the station we are receiving is from Medford, Oregon. We are moving the Volt out of the mine to get better reception.

May 24 – Housekeeping. We have improved the chicken pen, with a place to give them food scraps. We are planning an outside pen to let them scrounge from the forest litter and save the feed stock. Started new shelving.

Radio. It appears that the country is recovering, but still the southern half is under a thick cloud. Reports from the Space Station predict that it will last no longer than a week before spiraling into destruction. In the meantime, it is sending all the information it can back to Earth. The pictures show a planet that looks almost like Venus, we are told, a uniform bright cloud layer, but with some clearing from about latitude 45 north, and just barely visible in Antarctica. It seems that Denver is now the new operational center of the U.S. government, as it is essentially undamaged and has plenty of power from the coal-burning power plants. Its only hazards are ash deposits from the erupting Yellowstone mega-volcano, but these are infrequent.

May 25 – Housekeeping. Shelves finished. Since the power is (amazingly) still on in the mine, we are keeping the Volt recharged and looking at DVD movies each evening. We don't have many, so we are spacing them out. When we work outside, we can play CDs and have music in the camp.

Radio. We are now getting good readings on the extent of the tsunami. For example, Washington, D.C. was leveled, but Monticello inland was above the water line. Massive efforts are being made to house the refugees, and as yet no firm count is given for fatalities. The number will certainly be above 150 million. We are also getting reports from around the world, but except for some ham radio contact and NOAA's South Pole station, nothing south of the equator. The Space Station saw the tsunami tear apart the Antarctic ice sheets and the McMurdo Sound station. The tsunami essentially destroyed all of Japan, almost all of Taiwan, and inland *in China for more than 75 miles. Russia appears to be unscathed, as is much of eastern Europe, but western Europe and the Mediterranean countries have been badly hit. Central India survived, but Bangladesh and coastal India were eradicated.*

May 26 – Housekeeping. It is getting cooler, so we are going to try to block the mine entrance with the Explorer. We will leave a narrow passage at the driver's side, and use the open door of the SUV to shut this gap. We are building a sort of chimney so we can have a fire right behind the SUV and still have the smoke go out past the right side roof of the SUV and out into the air. We are collecting wood.

Radio. Janet Napolini is now reporting from Denver. This report was from the National Center for Atmospheric Research (NCAR) and it was a doozy. A team of scientists has run a model predicting a catastrophic cooling of the Earth for one-and-a-half to four years, depending on how efficiently the oceans can remove the dust and sulfur from the air. This epoch could set in as soon as two weeks. It will be devastating to all life on Earth. Immediate efforts must be made for survival, including domestic and wild animals and seeds, with mines and caves stocked with food. However, nothing the government can do will protect even a tiny fraction of the existing population.

Then the president came on. He said that this was a good time to make peace with your God and your neighbor, for almost all of you will be dead within weeks. We will do all we can to make sure that our civilization and the Earth's terrestrial ecosystem will survive, with gratitude for the seed and genetic repository already built in the European arctic in anticipation of a catastrophe like this. All mines and caves are now appropriated by the government for this purpose, and they will be protected by the military with orders to use lethal measures to protect them, if necessary. Theologians emphasize that catastrophe is part of nature, not God's vengeance, and similar events have punctuated the Earth's history, including a similar event that killed all the dinosaurs. But from the wreckage 65 million years ago evolved mammals that became humans and dinosaurs that became birds. Your creator will value how you handle your hour of trial. God bless you all.

We then had a meeting and modified our plans for surviving a very cold, extended period. The wisdom of Ken moving most of our group to the ocean and hopefully warmer conditions now looks like genius. We all hope they find food and shelter in what is surely a devastated plain.

May 27 – Housekeeping. We modified the water coming out of the mine spring so the chickens could get to it after we built a small cistern for our own needs well upstream of the chickens. The smell of the chickens is becoming strong, and if we are going to be trapped in here with them, we had better get them farther from the cave mouth. We are searching for suitable parts of the mine.

Radio. The Space Station is providing good data on the atmosphere. It seems that the sulfuric acid in the stratosphere has stabilized, and is no longer rising. It is also clear from the cloud tops that there are violent storms on both sides of the equator. This is good, according to the latest NCAR briefing. There is almost continuous radio chatter, but we are too busy to listen to it all.

It does appear that the biggest U.S. caves are being used to house animals, with enough food to last three years on lean rations. Each of these caves is to have a contingent of young protectors and animal care specialists, mixed male and female. Other caves, such as

Colossal Cave in Arizona, are being stocked for people.

May 28 – Housekeeping. We have moved the shelving back farther into the mine to protect it better. We have to anticipate that despite our resources, we ourselves may not survive. But if the Eureka team survives, this stuff may be vital. We are thinking about how we can maximize the chances for the chickens to survive.

Radio. Nothing much new, except that the government has been moved yet again to "an undisclosed location." Rioting and looting is occurring in the southeastern states as the constant cloud and dropping temperatures are shredding the social fabric. Westerners appear more resilient, and everybody is preparing their own caves, mines, and tunnels. Power plants are preparing for the worst, especially if cooling waters freeze.

May 29 – Housekeeping. We have rebuilt the mine fireplace. It now smokes less. Moving a lot of wood inside. Sheldon is estimating wood use for three years. We also are working on a way to restart a fire, if it goes out. Somehow we forgot matches, and since nobody smokes any more, only a few tired paper matches are here. We are keeping them scrupulously warm and dry, along with tinder and a wind-up flashlight.

Radio. Lots of chatter about preparations for the cold. Daily temperatures seem to be dropping even faster in Russia and northern Europe and Canada than in the United States. However, the long days and high sun angles are keeping temperatures generally above freezing during the days.

May 30 – Housekeeping. We have redone the chicken pens, and split up the feed so that some of it is very hard to reach through a narrow passage. Thus, even if we are gone, some chickens will get enough food to last years and, as long as the spring flows, some *will survive. We are not making that choice yet until we see how things progress.*

Radio. Word from the Space Station is that they must eject the Soyuz spacecraft to higher orbit because they are losing altitude significantly at each pass. A volunteer has been chosen for this suicide mission, which is not difficult because the team left on the station will probably have a pretty horrendous demise as it re-enters and burns up. Somehow despite the seriousness of the entire nation, the calm courage of these astronauts has hit a chord, and their attitude is being more and more copied among the population. Rioting appears to have subsided. Cold is getting extreme in the northern latitudes, but it has not dropped south yet.

May 31 – Housekeeping. We have greatly added to the air barrier around the Explorer, jamming wood and pine needles into every crevice except the driver side door, which we keep as our entry.

Radio. Massive migration of Canadians into the United States is occurring, with the borders now totally open. Good for us! I guess we add "and the cold" to the "tired and poor." Whole sections of the country are now being evaluated for shelter possibilities. The question of who is to be saved is now the big question. A choice has to be made, and it appears that people are to be given a priority number, based on scientific and technical expertise, youth, and health, including lack of drug use, chosen as much as possible to preserve existing families. Professors at small colleges with modest income and educated wives suddenly find themselves high on the list. Diversity is to be maintained at about the same level as the current U.S. population. No value is to be given on wealth, but a lot of very rich hedge fund economists are pushing hard to have economics included as a science. So far, the president is holding firm.

June 1 – Housekeeping. It is starting to get very cold outside despite the sun, which is somehow hazy and weak. We can still hear the massive eruptions of Mt. Shasta, but the plumes are generally going east. The Explorer has a DVD player for rear seat passengers, and we will probably stop using the Volt, because in the evening it is bitterly cold outside. The Explorer maintains its warmth, and we keep the fire going day and night, taking turns to watch it all night.

Radio. More of the same. Now NCAR is talking about Siberian highs and descending bitterly cold air, beyond anything ever known in the lower 48 states. We are accepting almost the entire population of interior Alaska, but the region around Juneau and Homer seem to be holding their own for temperature.

At that point Veronica's journal entries ended. It was clear that her group did not realize the threat of carbon monoxide emitted by the Explorer into a closed-air space and died peacefully listening to a CD, because there was no DVD screen in the driver's position.

All sat in silence, stunned by the unlikely demise of the mine group even before the intense cold and snow would have made their lives miserable. However, one result was that there was a lot of food that had not been used up.

7. FOOD

The next day, everyone turned out to finish constructing the greenhouse. It looked like a total disaster, with part glass and part translucent plastic. However, it was large – almost 60 feet long and about 15 feet wide – with sloping and nearly transparent panels facing southwest.

The group cultivated two raised beds – one on each side of a central walkway – which took almost three days to fill with mud (when available) and sand when mud was not available, and some of the sandy human waste from the sub-cellar of the hospital. They modified the outdoor latrines to make extraction of waste easier. Ken's team built a fireplace at the lower end, and the heat (and smoke) passed through the length of the greenhouse, which was sloped uphill. The smoke also showed a lot of air leaks, which they plugged as best they could.

The group had quite a ceremony on July 4, when the first seeds were planted. The rule was to use no more than half of any seed stock. The purpose was not to make food to eat, but to generate additional seed stock for next year. The food they had would last another winter, with important additions from the chickens. At the far end, they placed one redwood burl in water and sand.

It was only a week later that the first sprouts appeared from the snow peas. Within a week, almost all seeds had sprouted, as the greenhouse was being maintained at nearly 75 degrees F – even at night by the fire. Everybody made a point to visit the greenhouse once per day or more, but in small groups to minimize the loss of heat. One particularly enthusiastic plant turned out to be cabbage that Ken had found up at the mine. The potatoes were late sprouting but were vigorous once they started growing.

Two weeks later, the redwood burl showed the first green sprout.

As soon as the greenhouse was completed, all teams turned to help Roger with his bedpan waterwheel. Numerous jokes were coined about this unlikely device, but in about two weeks, they built the wheel and mounted it on the steel shaft. Roger constructed a flume, and the wheel turned easily and quickly from the first moment.

Much thought had been put into how to get the generator turning fast enough. The final design was based on the abundant tire rims lying in the mud, with nylon ropes as power transfer units. Ken's team built a shed for the generator. It had to be waterproof and high above the small ditch. This turned out to be the most difficult part of the effort, as a week passed while they tried various methods for waterproofing the shed.

Another team was putting up low poles and stringing a short transmission line using the abundant wire that was always lying around. Lacking a voltmeter, Roger had no real idea of how fast the generator had to turn in order to produce roughly 110 volts. He hooked up a fluorescent light fixture from the hospital to test it, and as each pulley was engaged the generator turned faster, but the bulb was dark. Roger was just about to ask for another fixture when he saw a flicker in the bulb. They added another set of pulleys, which took almost the entire afternoon, but when hooked up, the generator lit the bulb instantly.

Roger's team was exultant, but decided to keep their success quiet. They hooked the generator to the transmission lines, lacking only a single connection.

Dinner that night was a pretty happy event, with the greenhouse showing the first signs a life. Father John said grace, and then one of Roger's team members connected the wires using gloved hands. Suddenly the room, which had been dim for more than a year, was brilliantly lit by four fluorescent bulbs. Cheers rang out, and congratulations were offered all around.

That summer, teams of three were sent out on a wider search for any living plants. They soon ascertained that there was life in the ocean but no real way to benefit from it. The first success occurred when one of the teams was walking past a massive bank of gravel that had been laid down in the tsunami and was currently being undercut by a stream. There near the ground and buried under what was originally 25 feet of sand, a green sprout was evident. Wading into the freezing snowmelt, two members dug into the bank and pulled out a fairly substantial root structure with a green shoot on one end. Showing it triumphantly to the group, several people immediately recognized it as an Oregon blackberry, a really resilient plant that had been invasive in this area. They immediately planted it in the greenhouse, and without losing a beat, it sent up two new shoots from the root.

Roger's team had by now set up a technology center in a corner of the main room. With the availability of 110-volt power, the radios in Ken's battery charge system were turned on. They received no signals, neither AM nor FM.

"That's bad news," said Ken. "I had hoped that there was an existing surviving organization capable of broadcasting."

Meanwhile the meteorological team had ascertained that the maximum temperature for the summer would rarely break 50 degrees F, and nights were close to or slightly below freezing. Ken continued, "It is going to be very hard to raise food in such conditions. The chickens won't last forever, even as we are trying to find other food for them. I wonder if there are any options we haven't considered. We have to have food."

Andrew, one of John's team members, spoke up. "We see signs of life in the ocean. I saw some seaweed washed up yesterday, and I wonder if we could use it to feed the chickens, and perhaps us? Also, we should build a boat and become fishermen – and fisherwomen," he added quickly.

"Who here has any boating or maritime experience?" Ken asked.

Andrew answered, "I have sailed a bit over several summers, and got my Boy Scout badge in boating."

"Andrew, or as I should say, Captain Andrew, select a small group of workers, and on to it," said Ken.

"How can we survey our options most efficiently? It is still hard to travel any distance. Could the boat help?" asked Ken.

"The best way to cover a lot of territory would be by air. I had a pilot's license once," said Roger, "but I let it lapse."

Ken piped up, "I practiced in sailplanes, but always with a pilot. I was able to fly it, but never took off or landed. Still, we are notably short of aircraft. There must have been an airport around here. Let's at least check it out."

The month of August saw progress on every front, with the greenhouse positively exuberant with vegetation, and a 21-foot-long sailboat taking shape near a sheltered part of the bay that still had some protection from the greatly eroded sandbar that used to protect the bay. The survey of the airport was surprisingly useful, with a lot of hardware found in a ditch just downslope from the airport. In a box, they found a spare engine, still sealed up. In another container, completely flattened by the collapse of a hangar, was a sailplane. Almost nothing was salvageable except a few pulleys and cables, but at least the shape of the plane was evident.

Roger and Ken were hard at work, scavenging with their teams, finding all sorts of junk. Using the model of the wing from the ruined sailplane, they wired together the frame. They were searching all the junk piles for wing coverings, when suddenly a call came out.

"The salmon are back!"

Everybody ran to the hospital site. Andrew was excited. "The Mad River is filled with salmon! We need to catch and smoke them ASAP."

The entire team went off to gather whatever they could. The sleds were pressed into work again, and they modified snowshoes to make nets for the salmon. There was no time left in the day, but on the next day, all but one of the teams (one was always left at the hospital with a rifle), trekked to the river. The flows had dropped as the low-elevation snows in the hills had melted, and they found numerous shallow channels full of salmon.

Ken's team hastily put together a major smokehouse. "Does anyone know anything about smoking salmon?" Ken asked. No response. "Well, it has to be not too hot, yet hot enough to sterilize, I figure."

For the next three days, they caught, gutted, filleted, and smoked salmon. Every evening, the teams slept where they were. Finally, by the fourth day, they gathered the last loads of smoked salmon, grilled and ate fresh salmon, and put out the fires in the smokehouses.

Contentment filled the refugees as they knew this winter would be better than the last.

8. NOT ALONE

High above the Mad River, seven pairs of eyes surveyed the desolation. They had no idea that the coast had been ravaged by the tsunami. They were counting on food and shelter. All they saw was an enormous wasteland, sandy and muddy where Arcata and Eureka should have been. Their food was low, their need desperate.

They had a terrible journey that had already killed one of them, who fell into a river from a snow bridge. Their survival was a fluke, as they were the base team of the Mexican Zetas drug cartel, given the task of cutting the drug supply lines of their adversaries. They had been holed up in an abandoned drift in the Iron Mountain mine complex, with easy access to the main south-north drug corridor – Interstate 5. With their excellent intelligence, they had already intercepted three shipments, killed the couriers, and stole the drugs. They had abundant supplies, electric generators, and their own water source in the mine.

They had been out of touch when, without warning, an enormous flood had come up the valley, wiping out Red Bluff and Redding, and almost reaching the mine at 1,500 feet elevation. With no communications, they had no choice but to stay put as the cold descended. Holed up deep in the mine, they waited. Periodically, they would try to leave, but it was cold beyond any belief. Then came the snows that totally blocked their entrance. In panic, with food running low, they finally dug out the entrance. Before them was a Central Valley covered with vast snowfields, and to the north, an erupting volcano. Because nothing was visible to the east or south, they decided to hike west, to find the coast, which they thought would be warmer and could support survival. They were all heavily armed, with rifles, pistols, and knives, but limited food.

After a miserable hike through heavy snow, and without proper clothing, they persevered. Two days ago, they came across a trail which revealed that many people were also heading to the coast. Carefully following the trail, they at last crested the ridge and came out of snow for the first time in 11 days. But their hopes were dashed as they saw the devastation. What had happened? Where were the cities?

"I see smoke," Carlos said. "There, near the coast, by the river. There may be people there. Maybe even women."

"Be ready," Juan said. No other words were needed. They all knew what to do. They had done it so many times before. They were the best.

The hike down to the plain was easy, as it was warmer and

the trail was obvious. When they came to the Mad River freeway bridge, the temporary wood span was still in place. There had been no reason to remove it. There they waited until dusk, then carefully crossed. On the far bank, just below the bridge, was a camp of sort, smelling of fish. A fire had been burning not too long ago in a sort of shed. Because it was deserted, and even had some scraps of smoked fish that had dropped by accident to the ashes, they stayed near there, out of sight in case the people returned. They kept a close lookout all night.

The next morning, they started to follow the trail south. The trail was obvious but awfully exposed. You could see someone on the road from miles away. They decided to creep below the roads, more secure but much harder going. They took all day to move the 10 miles toward what they had hoped would be Eureka from their California AAA highway map. Dusk was falling when they dimly saw a small fire burning near a large pile of debris. They hid below the road, planning to reconnoiter that night.

9. FIRST HUMAN CONTACT

Andrew and Alice were seriously in love. However, while there was no way Alice was going to get pregnant in such conditions, physical affection was becoming an important part of their relationship. With fall approaching, they would soon find it harder and harder to slip away, and the dormitory had essentially no privacy. Tired and satisfied from the work of the last four days, and having finally packaged all the smoked salmon into the old refrigerator, they slipped away for a few minutes, walking down to the roadway where there was a dip that would hide them from view of the hospital. There, looking out across the surf line, they held each other, delighting in the feel of their bodies together.

Andrew turned to kiss Alice's waiting lips, and saw motion in the distance. Any motion was simply unknown these days in this desolation, so he froze immediately. Men were creeping toward them, under the lip of the road, hiding as they were. They were still about a half mile north, but even in the dim light, he could see what looked like rifles. The look on Andrew's face stunned Alice, when he touched her lips with his fingers for silence. He motioned that they should crawl south until they reached the place where the stream had cut a trench from the hospital to the ocean. Climbing into the ditch, they could cross the road unseen because the road had been washed away at that spot. Once around the corner of the hospital, they ran and met Ken and others lounging outside and enjoying the last light of the day.

"Men, several carrying what appeared to be rifles, are creeping toward us below the lip of the road, about a half mile north," Andrew said with fear and urgency.

For a second, everybody was stunned. "Into the refuge, now! Guys and girls, get weapons of any sort, but especially bring the rifles," said Ken.

Regretfully, two were only .22 caliber rifles, one was David's own .30-30 rifle, and one was Ken's scope-mounted .30-06. The weapons were distributed in an instant, and soon Roger, Ken, David, and Andrew had rifles, while Alice and Ginger had .38 pistols.

Ken motioned them to climb up into the debris pile to have a view down in different directions. Alice was to guard north and east, along the east hospital wall, Ken and Roger guarded west and northwest. David, the best shot, traded his short-range lever-action .30-30 for Ken's .30-06, and crawled over the debris until he was lying down almost over the ruined southwest corner of the hospital, close to where the fire was kept burning to heat the greenhouse.

In the refuge, everyone was given a weapon, some of which were just sharpened rods, knives, anything. Ken said, "If we fail, you must swarm them regardless of cost, or we will be eradicated." They arranged themselves in the darkened ruined corridor west of the main entrance.

Carlos's team had now reached the road directly between the hospital and the coast. The small fire was easily seen, burning next to a junky-looking structure. About 150 yards to the southeast, a low pile of debris and tree trunks would allow a good view of the south wall of the building where the fire was burning. Carlos took Roberto and Manuel, scrambled down into a small wash, and crawled along the road edge about a half mile south of the structure with the fire burning. There they crawled to the debris pile, and now had a good view of the compound.

There appeared to be a low wall that had not been destroyed. Several other structures were against that wall, showing some organization. Still, the structure and its trapped debris pile was large – 100 yards or more long and extending perhaps 20 feet into the air. It was hard to see more because the light was failing due to the setting sun.

No one was seen moving around. Carlos hoped someone would come to tend the fire, but nothing stirred. Carlos, Roberto, and Manuel arranged themselves to have good firing positions should anyone come out, and they waited. They planned to get closer once night had fallen.

High on the southwest end of the refuge, in a maze of debris, David had a good view of the debris pile used by Carlos's gang. Even though the light was fading, he could see three of the Zetas crawl to the pile, never suspecting that David at his high perch could see them until they were directly behind the debris. Still, the woodpile designed to heat the greenhouse used large pieces of wood that would burn all night, and it gave a flickering light over the scene.

Suddenly he heard a rustle behind him.

Rolling over, he saw that it was Alice stealthily crawling up. She said, "John wants to try to resolve this peacefully. He will make his move soon, but he needs to know what you can see up here." David gave her the rundown. "I spotted three people with rifles about 150 feet away and hiding, and the ones by the road are so far quiet." Alice crawled away.

About 10 minutes later, John's voice was heard loud and clear.

"We do not know who you are or what you want, but we do know you are all armed and stealthily approaching our refuge. We know that there are three of you only 150 feet or so away from me right now, behind that debris pile. We demand that you leave this vicinity or we will be forced to defend ourselves using lethal force. We are willing to give you some food to assist you in leaving, but if we see you again, we will shoot to kill without warning. We will take no action for 30 minutes so you can decide."

Carlos immediately zeroed in on the essence. "They are scared of us and want to bribe us away. I expect their threats are hollow. Roberto, you have the best English. Let's get their food and try to get a hostage at the same time." A short discussion followed.

Roberto replied loudly, "We are only trying to protect ourselves against bandits. We have no reason to hurt you. We would appreciate some more food as we are trying to get to our friends south of here. Please give the food to us, and we will immediately leave. We pledge our honor that no harm will come to the courier, and in return we will tell you about another group we fled from three days ago just north of here."

John, Roger, and Ken, with some of the students, considered the situation. John said, "This is a ploy to get a hostage. I am not willing to risk any of our people, but we can test their behavior by pitching out some food. Can anyone throw food that far?"

Roger piped up, "We could throw them a line with food attached to the far end, and let them reel it in. Then let's see their response."

John shouted out, "We are going to send you a line with enough food attached to get you at least 100 miles south. Then we ask you to leave and head south."

Nick, one of the Newman students who had a good throwing arm, went inside and began to collect some of the salmon into a hospital basket. They really regretted giving up 10 pounds of smoked fish, but they could cook more.

John attached a small section of a steel corner angle to suture thread, and Nick pulled the food to the edge of the pile. He crawled to the edge of the seats in the mini outside auditorium used in the daily briefings, and coiled the suture to allow a clean throw.

Without thinking about it, he lifted from his crouch to make the throw, and pitched the angle iron as hard as he could. It actually sailed over the debris pile where Carlos was hiding. Roberto crawled over, snagged the suture, and pulled. A basket started sliding across the area. It seemed reasonably heavy. When it was safely behind Carlos's debris pile blind, they opened the basket. Smoked salmon, perhaps 10 to 12 pounds of it.

Carlos smirked, "They are not stupid, but we now know where

they are in the structure. They are near the end of that structure with the fire at the far end. There is enough light. Manuel, get the rest out north of the pile, and then come around the end. I want all those who show outside the pile shot when I whistle. We will provide heavy automatic cover fire into the same region, and then charge in."

In about 20 minutes, Roberto raised to his knees and heaved the iron angle back at the refuge. "Give us five more pounds, and we will have enough," he yelled.

John said, "They are planning something. Let's accept but be ready. They may have weapons we don't know about, like Molotov cocktails. Whoever tries to send the line back will be at risk. I don't want to lose anyone."

Nick said, "Look, I can do it and stay low. Let's say 'yes' and be ready."

John replied to unseen menaces, "You are taking too much of our food, but we will give you five more pounds. We have little left. Throw the line back to us and we will send you the line back in a couple of minutes with the food."

John pulled the basket and re-filled it. Ken crawled higher in the debris above the entrance, and hid. Alice and Jonathan took pistols and covered the north and east wall, but it was so dark they couldn't see much.

"We are ready," said John. Nick crawled out of the shelter of the greenhouse, rose to his knees and pitched the iron angle. It easily reached Carlos's debris blind. But as soon as Nick had raised himself in the throwing action, Carlos sounded the whistle. A single shot erupted from the east wall, a totally unexpected direction, and Nick collapsed. Suddenly, AK-47 fire sprayed the entire face of the refuge.

Roberto stood to better direct fire at the entrance, and David dropped him with a single shot. Carlos ducked into cover, cursing in Spanish. He hauled the basket toward himself, and opened it to find pieces of concrete. Furious, he backed away, and in the dark David could not get a clear shot. Carlos reached the road, and joined Manuel and three others. In a minute, Juan came around the road end and dropped into the depression. I got one of them, but how is Roberto?"

"Dead," Carlos snarled. "Manuel, there is a lot of wood piled up. Start a fire on the northeast side where the wood is piled. We are going to smoke them out. Juan and the rest will give us cover from the blind in front of their holes."

Ken and Roger met to consider what to do next. Ken said, "If we stay in here, they will continue to trap us and eventually think of some method to kill us. Roger, I am not going to ask anyone else to do this, but I will travel east until it is dark away from our fire. I'll sneak down the creek channel and climb into their blind. I believe they will come back to it. David got one, so there may be weapons still there because it would be hard for the others to pull the weapons away without us seeing it, because the body is draped across the face of the debris pile and visible to us. I have the .30-30, and Roger, take a .38 pistol and cover me from one of those depressions in the sand east of their blind."

"In your dreams," said Roger. "Let's go before they can plan something new."

In about 10 minutes, Ken and Roger were at the debris pile near Roberto's body, hardly visible even to John and the anxious students at the entrance. They could see Roger carefully pull away the AK-47 while not disturbing the body.

Almost 40 minutes passed, and then suddenly light appeared from the east wall of the refuge, back near the northeast corner. Someone was setting fire to the enormous debris pile caught by the hospital's largely collapsed walls. Ken motioned to Roger, who froze in fear over what this might do to the refugees. He motioned to Ken to move back, but Ken stopped him. "There's tons of sand against the wall, and the wood is partially buried in it. Trust the students to take care of things."

Turning back and looking south, Ken spotted motion at the very edge of the channel about 200 feet away. Two people were crawling toward them, keeping very low. They had covered their faces with some dark cloth, so they were almost invisible in the night. When they stopped, it was hard to pick them out of the gloom, but then they moved again, closer, closer. When they were about 30 feet away and protected from the view of the refuge, they got to their hands and knees and began to move more quickly. Ken and Roger took careful aim, with Roger setting the AK-47 in a single shot mode (rarely used by Zetas who liked massive overkill). Ken tapped Roger, showed a thumbs-up, and then both fired simultaneously. The shots almost sounded like a single shot, but very loud. The two figures dropped as one – dead.

Another single shot followed from somewhere on the debris pile.

"Whatever is going on in the debris pile will keep the bandits occupied," said Ken. "I want to go down to the place below the road where they are hiding, and perhaps we can catch another."

The fire from the debris pile was now pretty intense, and in the flickering light what looked like packs and bundles were stacked in the cover. Roger and Ken grabbed all of them, dragging them into the ditch and up the channel, and back to the blind. They stacked them in full visibility of the refuge's front entrance, picked up the three AK-47s, and then ran back as fast as they could because the increasing light of the fire made crawling dangerous. Without incident, they made it to the entrance. The door and glass window had been shredded by the original fusillade.

"What is happening on the debris pile?" Ken asked anxiously.

"Alice got the one that started the fire," John replied. "The other students have blocked up the fireplace to keep out most of the smoke. The fire is not spreading very fast, and it seems to be going out in some parts."

"Who is still on the roof?" Ken asked. "David is in the southeast corner with the .30-06, Andrew has a .22 caliber rifle, and Alice has the .38 caliber pistol," John replied. "Let's get two of the AK-47s and add another student. We just grabbed all their supplies, and they can't get to them without being seen. Their own fire will keep the place lit until morning. Our worst vulnerability is the debris pile approached from the north face via the roof. Do we have all the sides covered? Where is Alice now?"

"At the southeast corner, with a good view of the entire east wall, thanks to their fire," replied John. "And likely Andrew is next to her but further in toward the center."

Back at the depression below the road, Carlos was beside himself with anger and despair. He had lost Manuel to a single sniper, two more ambushed at the blind, and now all their supplies were gone – their ammunition, their water, but especially their food. They had nothing. They would starve in days, and the gang in the debris would win.

Carlos gathered his shaken troops. "We have no choice but to destroy them tonight, while it is still dark and their refuge is on fire. The only way is across the debris pile from the northwest, where it is still in shadow. We will go together, with me leading. Keep low, and kill swiftly. We have certainly killed some of them already, and they continue to cower in their hole. The smoke will drive them out, and we can pick them off from the roof."

David saw movement first, over on the western debris pile, but no shot was possible. "They are coming," he said to Mark, one of the students, "and they are at the western edge of the debris pile where it is darkest." Mark crawled back and told Ken.

Carlos and his crew were making good progress. There was no sign of any opposition in the direction of the fire, which had flared up again and could be causing serious problems inside the structure. By sticking to the western edge, they were now only about 50 feet from arriving above the entrance. Then he saw motion. There was someone lying behind a concrete slab facing north, and the Zetas had flanked him to the west. Carlos motioned to his crew who came up to him, rifles at the ready. They crawled behind a concrete slab, pushing aside sand to make a concealed firing pit. Very cautiously, Carlos raised his rifle at full automatic and blasted the figure. The figure crumpled and then dropped, but at that moment a blast came at them from the right side, with multiple AK-47s sweeping their position. Carlos and one of his crew died immediately, while the one farthest north laid down his own barrage.

The gunfire from the northernmost bandit revealed his position, and Mark sprayed a volley of bullets that pocked the sand depression in which the bandit was crouching.

Silence. Only the crackling flames. Then a whimper.

Cautiously, Ken crawled toward Carlos, who was clearly dead, and then he spied another member of Carlos's crew lying on his side, doubled up, with his emptied AK-47 lying behind him. With guns drawn, they all approached the lone figure as they were anxiously scanning to the north for additional bandits. None. Father John came up, and knelt beside the bandit. "Madre de Dios," he moaned. John said, "Move away," and in Spanish started to talk to him. Soon, he began to administer the Catholic last rites because the bandit obviously was mortally wounded. About 15 minutes passed, and then John dragged a cloth over the bandit's head.

"Dead. It's over. There are no more, Father John said. "They were part of the Zeta cartel designed to intercept other cartels' drugs along Interstate 5, working from a well-equipped mine hideout. That's how they could survive the cold. But as their food ran out, they had to flee to the coast where they thought it would be warmer and could find food. They didn't know about the tsunami on the coast. They were on the verge of starvation and acted in the way the Zetas always act – maximum force."

Ken and Father John picked up the riddled dummy they had placed as bait, now full of holes. All hands turned out to snuff out the last of the fires, which had not been burning all that well in the wet wood, much of which was partially covered with sand.

A day of remembrance was decreed for Nick. Moving tributes and many tears. They then decided that the debris pile used by the Zetas would be the most suitable grave. They rearranged the pile and constructed a cross from the buried wood. Father John made a priest's stole out of the still-abundant hospital gowns, stained it purple with ink, and said the Catholic Mass of Burial.

"There are so few of us left," thought Ken. "Are we the last people alive on Earth? I hope not."

They buried the Zetas at two sites – each about a mile from the refuge in the area below the road they used to sneak up to the refuge. Simple crosses were assembled, but a rosary was draped on the Zeta who had confessed to Father John. They thought that this might deter future attacks. At least now, they were all well armed.

Aware that Father John was seriously depressed by the loss of Nick, Ken came up and said, "Father John, this was not your fault. None of us knew how well armed and desperate they were. In other circumstances, what you proposed could have worked with no lives lost." Father John responded, "Thanks, Ken, but as I told my students earlier, from now on, just call me John. It hurts less that way."

10. SUMMER

The next morning, the group decided to commit a full day to discussion about proposed work for the rest of summer. This year there was a summer, of sorts. It was cool to cold, but at least above freezing. The briefing was divided into three parts, corresponding to the focus of the teams.

Ken's team was responsible for weather and climate, including temperature measurements, analysis of sky conditions, ocean tides and ocean levels, trenches for evaluation of permafrost, wind and rain records, and agricultural and ecological restoration. The team members also were responsible for the wide-ranging scouting trips to detect the presence of surviving vegetation, as well as operation of the greenhouse.

Roger's team, which often borrowed people from Ken's team, was responsible for technology. They were tasked with the detection and rescue of tools, hardware, the construction of buildings, and preservation of lights and heat. They did daily scouting trips to all areas that might have equipment, especially the eroding oceanfront where so much of the debris of Eureka had been dumped by the tsunami backflow. Recently, they had added the local airport that housed small planes and general aviation. The main airport was still too far away.

John's team was responsible for social programs, collecting and preparing food, medical assistance, social welfare, education, and amusement. They were also responsible for the scouting teams that searched out food resources and maintaining the chickens. They worked with Ken's team to try to enhance the food via the greenhouse, but usually little was available because most plants were being grown for seed stock. The exception was snow peas that were doing exceptionally well, and having delivered an excellent seed supply for next year, provided some fresh greens.

Ken's meteorological team reported first.

"There are signs that the Earth is returning to a new normal, but a much colder one. We have about the climate right now formerly seen at Homer, Alaska. The sea is continuing to lower, probably because of the building up of massive continental snow sheets. Fall and winter will be bad, and occasionally brutal in cold snaps of limited extent, but nothing like the cold we experienced last fall and winter. Still, we are puzzled as to why we are not warmer. I believe the reasons are tied to the snow cover, which reflects more light back into space, and the fact that the sulfate, as shown by the orange sunsets, has not gone away. It is possible that continuing sources of sulfur are being emitted into the stratosphere from either the impact crater, which I doubt because it is at sea level, or more probably, volcanoes. Shasta continues to erupt, but at less intensity.

"Agriculture is going to be very difficult here, especially since we are having poor luck getting plants to form seeds. The exceptions are snow peas and potatoes. We are finding a few more plants, including finally a swatch of grass root material recently uncovered by the spring floods. It has no green on it at all right now, but it may recover in the greenhouse. Other plants, including ocean reeds and rushes, have little use for us but they may be useful for the chickens. If we are going to have to rely on agriculture to support us long term, we would do better in warmer conditions farther south."

Roger had a lot of news to report.

"With the waterwheel and 110-volt power, we are well along in getting a real workshop with power tools. This will make all construction easier. It is already clear that we are going to have to increase the power, perhaps by using more bedpans." Just then an undercurrent of ribald jokes broke out, including what crappy power it would be. "But the big news is we have just found an intact VW bug upside down at the edge of the ocean surf line. I want all of us to drag it out tomorrow. We have already shown that there is a lot of gasoline preserved in the underground tanks of the gas stations. We have plans to make the VW into an all-terrain vehicle and go back and get the heavier stuff still left in the mine. Finally, we are looking hard at the wreckage at the airport. We have already found an engine not badly damaged and a flattened sailplane container that was preserved under the collapsed hangar wall but then pinned by the sand. We have not yet been able to excavate it."

John let David and Alice handle their news.

"Good news on the food front," David began, "the additional food from the mine has helped, and we have just uncovered a new cache of goods from the supermarket. We have until now been looking downslope and finding scattered cans, but the tsunami first pushed upslope, and a bunch of stuff was preserved when the east wall fell."

As an example, Alice pulled out a tin of olive oil and a bottle of soy sauce. "Something to go with the snow peas," Alice piped in, laughing.

"Good to hear laughter again," thought John, who was still fighting depression at the loss of Nick and the tragedy of the Zetas.

Alice continued, "We are convinced that the sea has not been badly damaged by the severe cold, based on the analysis by Ken's team, and we are continuing with Roger's help on the sailboats. We are building two at once so there is at least the possibility of rescue if one goes down. Our first task will be to harvest seaweed, especially the kelp that we can see off shore. We are assured it is nutritious and can help feed the chickens."

After the briefing a better-than-usual lunch was served, and everyone went down to see Roger's VW. It took three days of digging in cold ocean waters, but on the third day, they were able to haul the VW out and onto dry land. Surprisingly, because the windows had been rolled up, it was fairly clear of sand inside. Roger's team immediately started to strip it, clean parts, and re-assemble it, while a second group built the specialized tool necessary to open the underground gasoline storage at two stations they had identified as being essentially intact.

"How can we make this into a snow machine?" queried Roger, "There is still a lot of hardware at the mine we could really use right now."

Much discussion, and lots of ideas were thrown out, but the best idea and easiest approach involved modifying the VW into a toboggan-like device, using skis on the front tires for steering and equipping the rear tires with paddles that would dig into the snow. By now, their machine shop had enough electric tools to be really useful, but lack of power limited how much could be done at one time. The upgrading of the waterwheel power plant was accelerated.

John's team was busily adding to their stock of smoked salmon, while boat construction teams, with assistance from Ken's team, were making good progress. They decided to build the boats one after the other, so the second could learn from the mistakes of the first. But it was still a great day, the last day in August, when the first hull was launched. The boat was roughly 36 feet long, with a raised bow to handle ocean waves. They hadn't yet constructed sails, but the boat was equipped with six oars – three on each side.

"All we need now is galley slaves and we are back to circa 500 B.C.," said Ken.

They found no need for galley slaves because everyone wanted to be on the first tour around the bay. They kept clear of the en-larged opening to the sea, because there was a lot of surf around it and strong currents. Roger had suggested that when the craft is ready for the ocean, it might be better to pull the boat along the shore to the ocean side of the spit to avoid the sandbar. The teams immediately started constructing the masts and sails, which would, of necessity, be made from the ever-so-useful hospital gowns.

The weather was now becoming distinctly colder, and rainstorms were starting to occur with some regularity. The outside dining hall and kitchen area was coming along nicely with new windows. It was much less dungeon-like than the inside hospital areas, but would not serve well when real cold came.

By the second week in September, the rear Volkswagen wheels with paddles were completed. They weren't pretty because the team still had no ability to weld, but with stainless steel wire support, they were operational. The group decided to do some quick work on the Mad River Bridge so that the VW could safely cross it. They were delayed by another rainstorm, which dropped some snow on the highest peaks rimming the plain.

Ken and Roger were itching to try the contraption out, so they brought in food and support teams, and on September 21, they were able to cross the river. They had built a trailer from spare parts, and modified it to be a toboggan if needed, so that the VW could now drive up to the snow line with a lot of people and supplies aboard. They finally found a spot where the road was starting to be snow covered.

"Hard as a rock!" exclaimed Roger. "The recent rains are freezing at night. We are not going to sink very far into this stuff."

"Sierra cement," remarked David. "I used to ski on the stuff."

They backed the VW onto the snow, and replaced the rear tires with the paddles. They sunk easily as far as the toboggan would allow, and with no problem at all they were back on the snow. The trailer likewise had its wheel removed, and soon the VW and trailer were up onto the ridge top near Willow Junction. Snow was becoming deeper, but it was still hard. Rather than descending down to the Salyer store area, they stayed up on the ridge and headed directly to the mine site without gaining or losing much elevation. The heavy snow and dead trees made it easy now, but the heavy vegetation would have made the trip impossible before.

The area around the mine was still somewhat cleared from the group's first visit in spring, because not much new snow had fallen, and the rain had melted some of the snow. They cleared the mine entrance and rolled out Ken's Jeep Cherokee. Without much hope, Ken turned on the ignition.

"There's some power left in the battery," said Ken. "Let's fill up the radiator and see if by some miracle it runs."

The little stream was still flowing out of the mine before being lost under the snow, so they collected some water for the radiator. However, the first attempt to start the engine gave a pathetic response.

"There are more charged batteries in the mine," said Roger.

They brought out two more batteries, and now the engine labored, but suddenly caught and ran.

"Well, that is a pretty useless exercise considering the snow shows no sign of giving up," said Ken.

Jonathan, who was usually the quiet one, said, "The VW rear wheel paddles have made a nice trench just the span of the wheels. I use to watch the series *Ice Road Truckers*. Perhaps we could put water in the ruts and drive out. The Jeep is a 4 x 4, and the snow is hard."

By now everybody was getting tired of walking around so much. Every scouting trip involved many miles, and it was hard to haul much stuff back.

Ken said, "I think we should stick to our original plan, use the VW and sled to get all useful stuff down to the snow-free road. Then let's come back and see what we can do. The ruts are indeed pretty hard, and the Jeep clearance is high enough to avoid the middle hump."

The haul from the mine was not as useful as before, because the really important stuff had been gathered in spring. Much that was there would not be useful soon – maybe never. The stash in the cave included a whole lot of cell phones, and other no-longer useful supplies. But two days later, they successfully drove the Jeep out of the snow by following the VW ruts. The hard sides of the paddle trench kept the wheels in the rut. By now, the soft spots in the wheel trench had been hardened with water taken from the mine spring.

For once, Ken looked positively sheepish. "I hate to even mention this, but I wonder if the Volt could be towed out on the sled. It still has some charge in its battery, which could help, especially since the Jeep has an extra set of tire chains. The Volt has a big battery, which would provide more light at night. It also has XM satellite radio, if that still works."

After much laughter and amusement, the task turned out to be surprisingly easy. The sled fit under the Volt and rested on the snow. The rear ties with chains were in the trench, and they hooked the Volt to the end of the VW. The Jeep left first, then the VW and the Volt, with everyone riding in one of the three vehicles. Moving steadily but slowly, they had to use the Jeep's winch only twice at places where it did not have enough traction to climb a grade. Still, a very tired but happy group finally arrived at the paved road late on the fourth day.

16

"Better boogie, folks," said Ken. "It is very cold, and I don't like the look of the approaching storm clouds. We may get snow at sea level with this one."

Getting across the Mad River Bridge in the dark was a trial; however, having headlights helped enormously. They finally arrived at the refuge around 10:00 p.m., to the amazement of the three people guarding the site. Wild celebrations ensued when the new vehicles arrived, essentially simultaneous with the first snowflakes. They backed the Volt up to the entrance as close as the stream would allow, making easier access. Because the cold was not yet extreme, they left water in the radiators but were prepared to drain them if the severe cold arrived. Still, compared to last year, the refugees were a lot warmer.

The next morning, about a foot of snow had fallen, but no extreme cold had followed. The entire plain looked pretty with all the mud covered up. The sound of the ocean waves seemed muted. The next storm three days later brought rain, and most of the snow melted. The group decided that the highest priorities would be to protect the newly built boats and to run the Jeep over to the market and really raid the new cache of cans and bottles east of the wall. Lots of people and tools were needed because they had to penetrate the collapsed wall to get to the good stuff. While they made a lot of detours to avoid mud, the Jeep arrived back with several hundred pounds of food. Regretfully, one of the biggest types was cat food of various kinds, hopefully destined for the chickens.

The chicken flock had thrived in summer, eating garbage and some feed enhanced with seaweed that had washed ashore and was chopped into small pieces. The new chickens were larger and healthier than their parents, and their egg production steady increased. John had segregated roosters from hens and partitioned off three groups of hens, each with one rooster, and a bachelor pad for the extra roosters. They wanted to prevent inbreeding, which can be a real problem in a small flock. Well-built coops were situated directly against the hospital's south wall, and the heat from the ever-burning fires for the greenhouse was directed into their area. The coops inside the first room were ready when needed, but the smell would be far more tolerable by keeping them outside as long as possible.

11. SECOND HUMAN CONTACT

Once the Jeep and VW had finished making trips, anticipating that there would be more snow soon and such trips would be impossible, Ken turned his attention to the Volt. The refugees had been charging the battery for three days whenever excess power was available, knowing that their stream and waterwheel could freeze at any time. Having the battery at maximum charge could be useful in the days ahead. They built a rough shed next to the outside chicken coop to cover the Volt for protection against the cold, and the heat of the ever-burning greenhouse fire was directed into it.

Thus it was almost an afterthought that more than one week since the return from the mine, Ken turned on the radio. AM and FM – nothing. Just on the chance, he flipped over to XM radio, and heard:

"....and the EOS satellite shows a slight reduction in the mid-latitude sulfuric acid cloud. This will enhance the warming. It won't be enough to avoid another brutal winter, but the weather will be far less severe than last year. We still have seen no sign of melting of the snow cover over the U.S., except on the West Coast, where up to 25 miles inland is now clear near Santa Maria, California. We lose satellite coverage below about Santa Barbara from the still-persistent cloud cover that extends as far as the EOS satellite can see into the Southern Hemisphere. This concludes the 3:00 p.m. climate report. We will be on the air again at 6:00 p.m.

"This is the Cheyenne Mountain Directorate near Colorado Springs, Colorado, at 104.85 W, 38.74 N. We are maintaining this service as long as the XM radio uplink and the EOS satellite allow, in the hope that there are still people able to hear this report. We continue to monitor all ham radio bands in hope of a response, including..." There followed a string of frequencies that meant nothing to Ken.

By now, everyone was running to the Volt, but by then the report had finished. Then without any introduction, classical music started playing. "Mozart's 20th piano concerto," exclaimed Ken, "One of my favorites."

Roger, ever analytical, said, "Keeping the channel always active increases their chances for someone to pick it up."

"I prefer to think that they are just into one of the most beautiful things that humankind has ever done," responded Ken, the hopeless romantic.

Three hours later, the entire group was draped all over the Volt for the 6:00 p.m. Mountain Standard Time climate report. It was so similar to the 3:00 p.m. report that it was probably a copy. But it was followed by a one-hour summary of all events from the time that members of the military, their families, and selected experts, including two from NCAR, and a few politicians, also with families, were hurriedly shuttled into Cheyenne Mountain, 2,000 feet underground, in the face of the first impact of the severe cold. It had caught everyone by surprise. They had calculated that it might last three or four years and allowed only 134 people in all, knowing that they could live that long on the stored food supplies.

During the cold, they listened with hopeless despair while their numerous links around the world started failing as resources froze, food ran out, and power sources failed. A few survived until what they hoped would be spring, only to find essentially the entire nation blanketed with heavy snow. They were trapped, and by June of year one, no links survived. They were alone.

Still, hoping for any contact, they kept the XM satellite link active, hoping that some warming would occur before they, too, ran out of food.

The next group meeting of the California refugees was scheduled for the following day after breakfast, but it convened indoors because the weather was becoming nasty.

Ken's meteorological team started. Jonathan gave the group report that day. "We are seeing a steady decrease in temperatures, but following the trend, it will never get very cold. Barring the cold incursions, it will be a cold but bearable winter. However, we expect the Siberian high over Canada to collapse onto us periodically in winter, hopefully with less impact than the severe cold we experienced. We also note that we have almost no permafrost left within a couple of miles of the coast. The retreat of the permafrost will greatly help vegetation."

Ken continued. "What we have learned from Cheyenne Mountain pretty much supports our conclusions. What is new is the continuing heavy cloud deck south of Los Angeles extending over the entire Southern Hemisphere for reasons unknown. However, it will continue to reflect sunlight back into space and cool the Earth. Thus it appears that the best place to grow plants is about the Santa Maria plain. I propose we consider moving part of our team there. But finally, how can we possibly rescue the Cheyenne Mountain people?"

Roger's team was next, buoyed by their successes. "We can sail or we can fly," stated Roger. Everybody was transfixed. Roger continued, "I told you earlier that we had found a Cessna engine still in its original crate and wrapped in plastic. Well, we have now excavated the sailplane container from under the collapsed east hangar wall, and it contains a two-seat sailplane, badly smashed. But I think that it could be repaired, mated with the Cessna engine, and fly with one person and some cargo, or even possibly a second person.

"I propose that we bring this all down here, and set up an extension to our workshop. Ken, you have a good digital camera and downloads to your laptop. We could take pictures and finally really see what is around us. I would propose that we use the plane, if we can get it to work, in conjunction with the boats so that there is both support and some possibility of rescue in case of a crash."

Ken spoke up, "It also, at least in theory, presents a way we may be able to reach the Cheyenne Mountain people, but it would push us to our limits. I still believe translocation to better climates, guided by what we learn from our flights, is the first priority, or we would be unable to feed 134 people."

The excitement was palpable, but Roger's team still had a report. Progress on the boats was slowed by the cold and the mine retrieval, which used almost the entire crew. But they would work during the winter on sails and rigging and try to be ready in spring to support whatever was planned.

John also raised the question of the social compacts. Encouraged by the progress of the refugees on all fronts, and longing to fulfill strong emotional ties, enhanced by the fears from the Zetas' attack, three couples had come to him wanting to be married. That raised the real possibility of children by next summer. John supported the idea, and proposed to have all three ceremonies at the same time. He even had thought of ways to get a bit more privacy for couples by subdividing Room 2 and moving some singles into Room 4, which was always the warmest.

The day chosen was October 12, Columbus Day, because they all considered themselves explorers in a strange land. No one was surprised to see Andrew and Alice, but the announcement by the quiet Jonathan and vivacious Jeanette was a bit of a surprise. Ginger and Seth from Newman always had been an affectionate couple.

12. THE COLD: YEAR 2

The really cold weather held off until November 3, but lasted a full four days. The estimated minimum temperature from the now calibrated thermometers of Ken's meteorological team estimated 111 below zero F for the low and 35 below for the high. These were temperatures that had been seen on occasion even in Alaska, so clearly things were getting better. The winter alternated between snow, occasional cold snaps, and by February a rainstorm. But the spirit in the refugees was completely different from the bunker mentality of the severe cold of the first year. The married couples looked ecstatic, the boat teams were busy at work, and other than in the cold snaps the airplane project was progressing. The motor was going to be mounted behind the pilot, where the second passenger would have been, to balance the weight. The propeller was on a long shaft that extended behind the tail assembly. All struts had been broken in multiple places, and a lot of work went on to find substitutes. The aluminum skin was a mess, and even when pounded, was wrinkled and torn at many spots. They were able to repair enough to surround the pilot and engine, and a place for cargo in front of the pilot, and the tail assembly could be repaired. But they were baffled about what to use for the wing fabric and the body structure from the engine to the tail. Finally, they decided on plastic trash bags, double thick, held together with sutures and medical tape. It looked like crap. But would it fly?

Ken's team took over the task of insuring that the XM signal was constantly being monitored. The weather reports were fascinating and confirmed their own measurements. The EOS satellite data revealed that the equatorial clouds were the result of massive storms as the cold air passed over the still-warm ocean water. It was also clear that EOS had identified sulfuric acid from ongoing volcanic eruptions, including Yellowstone National Park, which had a massive eruption at the time of the impact.

Finally, on March 23 of Year 2, the plane, which had generated all sorts of names – most of which were based on the use of trash bags – finally was christened "The Gossamer Phoenix," and was moved by hand to the airport site. Ken cleared the runway of debris with the Jeep acting as a plow. Some sand remained, but not enough to hinder takeoff. Finally, the fuel pumped from the gas station tanks was brought to the airport. They decided against mixing the two tanks present at most stations, because they were not sure which had the higher octane.

The engine started but at first didn't run well on any of the fuels. However, they selected what they thought was the best fuel and tinkered with the carburetor and timing, and eventually the engine ran with good power. The final test was 12 hours continuously.

After much discussion, Ken was chosen as the designated pilot. His knowledge of physics and brief experience in sailplanes, combined with the fact that he was much lighter than the husky Roger, were the deciding factors. Everyone had lost about a quarter of their original body weight in the past two years, it turned out.

They conducted the first tests up and down the runway, with two extra bicycle wheels lowered on each side to stabilize the single main landing wheel directly under the pilot. There was also a small wheel at the tail to prevent the propeller blade from touching the ground. After more testing, some weight was added in front of the pilot, and the two wing flaps (absent in the original sail plane) were made larger. Finally, Ken simply could not resist, and on a clear cool morning with little wind 10 days later, he got the OK from Roger to fly. Roger said, "For God's sake, stay low so you could survive a crash!"

Ken increased the power, and the plane smoothly left the ground. He had actually too much power, and had to cut back a lot until the plane was flying smoothly. It was not designed for high speed. He was already about three miles out when with some trepidation he tried a turn. It took a while to get it right, but with the rudder and a wing tip, he was flying back to the airport. His confidence was increasing by the minute. Deep inside, his hidden "little boy" was fully engaged. So as he approached the airport, he dropped down to about 30 feet and buzzed the crowd. He continued to fly around for 30 minutes, and then decided to try the critical maneuver – landing in one piece.

It was actually easier than he thought. He cut down power until the engine was barely turning over, and the plane lost altitude smoothly. His altitude was too high on the first pass, and on the second, but on the third pass he flew onto the runway, cut the engine, and then realized there were no brakes. He happily realized that he had a lot of runway to work with, along with a buffer of some sand, at which he aimed, in the same way that runaway trucks used gravel-piled escape ramps on mountain highways. The right helper wheel caught at the end and spun the plane to the left. But all was well, and he cut the engine.

"Show-off," chided a grinning Roger, while pounding him on the back. "We thought you were trying to land when you buzzed us."

Jonathan was also of slight build and asked if he, too, could be a pilot. So Ken and Jonathan trained on the airplane, modifying flaps and tail structure, strengthening the balance wheels on each side, and adding the most rudimentary brake imaginable – a pivoted rod with a wooden shoe at the end that could be dragged on the ground. Jonathan incessantly practiced taxiing and turning, and Ken was able to take him on flights by jamming him into the cargo space in front of the pilot and describing what he was doing and why. Finally, Jonathan was allowed to go solo, and landed safely on his first attempt.

By early April, both boats had been completed and were routinely sailing up and down the protected part of the bay. Ken's meteorological teams had identified that a certain storm pattern would precede three days of calmer winds and rising atmospheric pressure, measured from the altimeter that the Jeep had carried. They chose a day, and both boats were carried out to the bay along the shore onto the ocean beach. They were pushed out over the modest surf, and everybody climbed in. The four people who sailed first represented almost every young person among the survivors, plus Cathy. Now it was Ken's turn to stand on the shore and anguish over the dangers involved. Yet hour after hour, they sailed back and forth, tacking and running with the wind. Finally, the first boat, which they named Peter, approached the opening of the bay. The boat pitched, but rode easily across the waves and into the bay. Ken though that the much wider bay opening caused by the tsunami may have made the crossing less fearsome than in prior years. The second boat, named Paul, followed, but came too close to shore and grounded. Three people hopped out and pushed it back into the bay. The audience on the shore was picked up and all sailed to the sheltered dockyard with much laughing and good cheer, plus some kidding about running aground. Still, they now had two boats and competent crews. Everybody knew that a new phase was about to begin.

13. SCHISM 2

Roger and Ken had made all the changes in the Gossamer Phoenix, including adding fuel cells and testing to see if the airplane could still fly well. By adding tanks both in front of and behind the pilot, they eventually were able to load about 40 gallons (about 240 pounds) of fuel aboard the aircraft and still take off. They couldn't land with that much fuel, and had to vent it during the trials, but the point was made. The Gossamer Phoenix could fly for as long as six hours at about 120 miles per hour and still have a 15 percent fuel reserve. With a more careful inventory of fuel, Ken identified several thousand gallons of high-octane gasoline in 14 old gas tanks.

Ken's camera was mounted below and in front of him, with the shutter release available at his right hand. His first test was just a local flight, to a point just north of a nice protected harbor at Trinidad Head, and from there to a coastal area south of Cape Mendocino.

The pictures were eagerly examined by everyone on the laptop computer, and Roger and David determined that Trinidad Head was a much safer location for the boats. Because the weather was still good, Ken headed south the next day, and saw another nice harbor that he thought might be Shelter Cove. After each flight, Ken and Roger made a detailed post-flight analysis, and it became clear to them that using the low glide path of the sailplane could save a lot of fuel.

It was probably pushing their luck, but when the third nice day dawned, Ken pumped a full fuel load and headed for San Francisco, 270 miles south. The view was almost exactly the same – a bare area close to the coast, and heavy snow on ridge tops a few miles inland. Ken noted the excellent harbor at Bodega Bay, and a bare section of roadway that could serve as a landing strip. There was little to show that the weather was any more favorable for agriculture than the Eureka area. The flight over San Francisco was stunning. The city was clearly visible as an enormous mass of debris – mostly concrete and steel. Amazingly, the tall towers of the Golden Gate Bridge still stood, but showed no trace of the roadway. However, in summary, the whole scene looked uncannily unchanged, possibly because there didn't appear to be much sand around. He turned back and made it to Eureka with 22 percent of his fuel left over. That evening everyone viewed his pictures, which were stunning.

In his post-flight briefing, Ken said, "Well, Roger, your team did a splendid job on the airplane. A few small rips were easily fixed, but my goal is unmet. I can see no region that would be any better than here for agriculture. I want to go much farther out next time. I propose we send the boats south with fuel to Bodega Bay, which has a good harbor and a road that would serve as a landing strip. I don't want to do thus until I get confirmation from Cheyenne Mountain that the weather has stabilized. Certainly this spring is warmer than last, but the ridges are still snow-covered, even south of San Francisco."

Everyone knew there would be serious risks involved with this journey, because they were committing both boats with 2,100 gallons of fuel, eight people, and Ken for a mission in which all sorts of things could go wrong, with devastating consequences to the group's survival. Preparations were ready by early May, and the boats set off for their farthest patrol ever. They were to go to Bodega Bay and clear the roadway for an aircraft landing. If this were not possible, they agreed on a signal to send Ken back; however, it would be at the very edge of his flight range. But if he could refuel, he could make it all the way to the Santa Maria plain that was mentioned by people from Cheyenne Mountain and still make it back to Bodega Bay.

One week later, the forecast was favorable, and two days before the flight the boats set off. The wind and waves were still significant from the storm that came through two days prior, but the boats rode well and the winds were pushing them south at a good speed. "Coming back will not be as easy," thought David.

They arrived at Bodega Bay in good time, and penetrated to the end of the bay. Ruined wharfs were still present and a hazard, but they found a landing spot. One road along the northwest shore of the bay was almost free of debris and had minimal sand. One day's work, and they were ready.

The next morning, at the scheduled time, they sighted Ken's airplane and gave him the "OK-to-land" signal by igniting road flares. The road was plenty long but slightly curved, and after a few test passes Ken landed in good shape. Refueling began immediately, while Ken had a cup of coffee. In 35 minutes, they pushed the airplane into position and Ken took off – sluggishly, however, because of the heavy fuel load.

The flight south was uneventful. Sadly, all the mountains behind Big Sur were heavily covered with snow, and the shore was steep with few if any bays. Finally the mountains seemed to relent and pull back, and an enormous muddy plain stretched to the snow-covered hills. "Somewhere up there used to be San Simeon," Ken thought, but no trace remained. He hoped it was just invisible under the snow pack.

Morro Bay was obvious because of Morro Rock, but everything else was swept clean. Ken saw a lot of sand inland, but nothing looked promising. Moving south, he saw two domes in a small canyon, surrounded by wreckage. He recognized it as Diablo Canyon Nuclear Power Plant. "I sure hope it shut down before the tsunami," thought Ken. Actually, either the president's warning or the impact earthquake would have triggered it automatically. With the dome structure intact, there should not be much radiation around after two years of cooling. However, there would be no way to test that theory. Coming across the hills south of where San Luis Obispo used to be, Ken realized that for the first time the low hills inland for miles had no snow on them. A large, sandy beach stretched before him just south of Pismo Beach, and there was the mouth of the Santa Maria River and the plain mentioned by people at Cheyenne Mountain. He spotted a trace of green near a creek, and he took pictures, then banked the plane to get a closer shot. Definitely there was green vegetation along an undercut creek bank, but no sign of people or any animals. Moving south, he saw another patch of green along the edge of a river channel, always an area that had been covered by sand, protecting it from the severe cold, and then brought to light and life by erosion. He turned, and headed north, noting that he now had a headwind.

His fuel was well into the 15 percent reserve as he passed over the Golden Gate Bridge with its two lonely towers but no roadway span. He throttled back and almost glided down to Bodega Bay, landing into a nasty crosswind. He got the plane down, but it skidded downwind onto sand. The left support wheel crumbled and the wing hit the ground hard. Ken cut the engine as the boat crews ran up. He climbed out of the airplane and said jokingly, "Well, I met the minimum criterion for a safe landing – I'm walking away from it. But I have some good news. I found some vegetation south of San Luis Obispo. I think we have found our second home."

It took only about an hour to fix the wing with some duct tape that was always present in Ken's Jeep, and now reserved for aircraft repairs. Refueling took another 40 minutes, and then Ken got ready to take off. This time he aligned his airplane roughly into the wind. It shortened the road runway but the strengthening breeze would aid lift. Gunning the engine, he cleared the dune in front rather more easily than he had anticipated and headed north. The boat crews were already packing up for the long trip back, largely into the wind. "Thank God we have two boats," thought Ken, "I would hate to rely on one in these rough seas."

Ken arrived at the Eureka encampment and touched down just as the sun was setting, to the enormous relief of Cathy, Roger, and everyone else. He was exhausted, but said immediately, "We have a new home. I saw vegetation!"

People were really not ready to celebrate until almost three days later, when the exhausted boat crews crawled into the harbor along the smoothest passage they had marked. They tied up the boats and almost staggered into their beds, not having slept much for three days.

That night, the wind kicked up and rain driven by wind slashed through the structures. Now no one really cared. All the birds were home, and with good news.

Only two days later, when everyone had recovered, Ken set up the laptop computer in Room 4 with its cheery fire and fluorescent lights. The waterwheel power station was in full operation again and, in fact, there was a bit too much water so they dug a diversion channel to control flows to the wheel.

Ken carefully went over every slide, one by one, taking enough time so each person could get an up-close view of the laptop screen. The brutal scenery of Big Sur and the snowy mountains gradually gave way to Morro Bay and then the Santa Maria plain. Using old road maps, they examined each area minutely. The first set of greenery was on Arroyo Grande Creek, which led past the poetically named village of Halcyon to flat fields just inland from the ocean. There didn't seem to be much sand on the fields, which looked dark in the pictures. One of the photos showed a straight road that could be used as a landing strip. Everyone was almost giddy with excitement. The first snow-covered mountains were many miles inland, and air from them would have to pass over coastal hills to reach their place.

Ken continued, "Farther south, all was sand, extending miles inland. The second patch of green was where the Santa Maria River cut through new sand banks just before entering the ocean, but the entire inland area was sand-covered.

"Farther north, I saw there was a small harbor that, according to the map, is called Port San Luis. It's protected from wind and waves. It's badly ruined, but there are parts of piers still standing. It would serve our boats well.

"That's the last of the photos," said Ken. "No more discussion today. Let's sleep on this one."

Sleep was the last thing on anybody's mind right then.

People broke for lunch in a joyous mood. Later, over in a corner, Cathy sat weeping copiously. Ken noticed, gave her a big hug and asked, "What's the matter?" Cathy leaned close to Ken and said, "In my heart I was afraid we would never see green plants again, and that we would have to live in a brown world. Now we found some, which verified to me that the Earth is still alive."

The next day the rain had relented enough so they could hold a regular meeting in the outdoor amphitheater.

"What are your thoughts?" began Ken.

"When can we move?" asked Jonathan.

The entire group cheered and clapped.

Jonathan and Cathy had really become the master gardeners, and they felt most keenly the difficult conditions, but clearly everybody was committed.

Ken looked at everyone, and said, "Well, that was short and sweet. The key will be the boats. They will have to transport people and tools to immediately get seeds into the ground for any chance of a harvest. I propose that Roger, who seems to know something about everything, lead the expedition with Andrew guiding the second boat with his pregnant wife, Alice, who would not be parted from him. Cathy and I will stay here with Jonathan, Jeanette, David, and one other volunteer to protect our base until we know you are secure. I am going to give you most of the firepower since we are reasonably secure here. Roger, take what you need to produce electrical power and build shelters. You'll probably be digging into the bank that faces southwest – just north of the Arroyo Grande stream.

"Once the boats are unloaded, send one back up here with the news and for more supplies as you understand your needs. Jeanette, give your two other redwood burls to Ginger, another competent gardener, since they clearly can't survive the winters up here. We will keep only the seeds that we know grow here, but make sure you have potatoes, snow peas, and chard."

The heavily loaded boats were riding low in the water. Eight people were making the trip, which was about all the boats could hold safely, while six stayed behind. Tarps made of garbage bags were used to cover parts of the boat to avoid swamping if they hit a heavy wave. The next morning, they set off.

Ken met with his team. "I believe we must make every effort to contact and then rescue the Cheyenne Mountain people. Reports indicate that they're starting to see a date when supplies will begin to run out, showing they can't last much beyond the next summer as long as the entire area near Cheyenne Mountain is snow covered. The fact that they are at an altitude of 9,500 feet just makes things worse. The cold is relentless."

Ken had by now a pretty good idea how far he could fly in calm weather. He had stretched the range to nearly 900 miles with the extra fuel tanks, but that wouldn't quite do it because it's 1,000 air miles to Cheyenne Mountain from Eureka. Then there was the question of landing and refueling. But they all huddled together and gradually hatched a plan. They would make the first run, and find a runway about 350 miles out, so the plane could go and return. Once that was found, they would make more trips, each dropping off fuel at this depot. Then they would from that site find a second site somewhere in western Utah near Wendover with a flat road, and repeat the process. Finally, from that last stop, they would fly to Cheyenne Mountain and, without landing, drop a message opening contact and letting them know that the California group could hear everything they put onto XM satellite radio. The first questions were if they could find or make a runway and if they had gasoline to fuel the plane. Without those, rescue was impossible.

Ken insisted on making the first flight. Taking off from Eureka and heading south before turning east to avoid the modest ash plume that now on occasion came from Mt. Shasta, he headed for Lake Tahoe. The ever so useful GPS was supplemented by AAA maps, and that part was easy. It was discouraging to see the entire valley still snow covered in mid-September, but an even bigger surprise awaited him at Lake Tahoe. It was frozen over. This had never happened before because of the lake's great depth, but now it was a 30-mile long expanse of snow.

It was eerie to fly over the essentially undamaged buildings of Reno in its blanket of snow, but it was then easy to follow Interstate 80 east. Finally, at a high pass that Ken guessed was Golconda Summit, he found what he was looking for. A stretch of

Interstate 80 had been swept clear of snow, and because daytime temperatures were probably above freezing in mid-summer, about a mile was almost entirely snow-free. There were some drifts he would have to avoid on landing. With great care, he buzzed the site twice and then touched down. Since he had enough gas to get back, he unloaded the emergency spare fuel from the front cargo compartment, and put the bright red cans next to the road. Without the weight, and with almost half of his onboard fuel gone, the takeoff was easy, using probably less than 600 feet of the road. On the way back, he carefully noted fuel use versus distance. He was getting better and better at using the sailplane's capabilities at low speed to extend range.

Three weeks later, the first boat returned to Eureka with just a three-person crew, including Andrew and Alice. Upon landing and joyous hugs, they reported that the Santa Maria location is perfect, much warmer, and on the valley floor, has wonderful soil once you scrape away a little sand. One crew is building shelters, a second under Roger is getting irrigation water, and a third with Linda and Ginger is planting crops. The banks protected the site, extending up to about 150 feet, and the southwest-facing slope near the bottom is distinctly warm.

"This place is perfect," said Alice. "Unfortunately the vegetation is just willows and some salt marsh rushes, but it is green. I have a request: Can we have some chickens? We have found enough debris to make an extensive pen, and even included some willow shoots."

"They won't last long," laughed Ken, "but take two separate flocks and two extra roosters. We can do with just the third flock."

Ken, Jonathan, and the team then explained what they had

planned for the Cheyenne Mountain rescue.

"God, that is so scary," said Andrew.

The next day, the boat was on its way with assorted technology, a massive load of smoked salmon, and other canned food stock to help them survive the upcoming winter. The southern team already was starting to search out canned food that survived the tsunami at the site of Arroyo Grande, a town a few miles inland.

"Be sure to get some kelp," Ken reminded them. "You are going to be on short rations, and I don't know how many trips you can make before winter sets in."

By early September, Ken and Jonathan were ready. They had identified another stretch of Interstate 80 west of Wendover, and after four flights they had 40 gallons of fuel stashed. Jonathan was lighter than Ken, and was chosen for this extremely risky mission. He had to fly all the way to the Wendover site without refueling. He would land there, refuel, and take off for Cheyenne Mountain, which is about five miles southwest of Colorado Springs. He would try to arrive around noon, and drop a roadway flare and, if necessary, a hand grenade (which one of the Zetas had in his pack) to make noise. Finally, when people were present, he would drop a message in a small parachute and head back to Utah. He would then refuel, essentially emptying that supply, and fly back to Golconda Summit or, if weather was favorable, all the way to Eureka.

Much thought was put into the message. Jonathan and Ken had modified the airplane so that one person could sit in the cargo space, cramped and cold, but as safe as the rest of the plane. The weight would cut down the range. So first they must ascertain that they had a place to land and that they could get gasoline at

Cheyenne Mountain for refueling. Even if they filled up at Cheyenne Mountain, they would have to stop twice for refueling to reach Eureka. Ken and the team set the standards by which the transfer would proceed.

Ken said, "We can help them, but they must help us. Our biggest lack right now is medical expertise. If anyone gets seriously hurt, or there are complications giving birth, they could die. I am going to request that the first person shuttled is a young M.D. with a family, and that they all come. Then we would want additional young families, each with special capabilities. My guess is that with all the fuel shuttling, we can make maybe three or, at the most, four person transfers before winter. What we need from them is good meteorology so we can make the best of the winds and avoid especially the volcanic plume from Yellowstone."

By September 12, they were prepared. The standard weather report from Cheyenne Mountain indicated a stable high-pressure ridge that would last a few days. They also reported that this summer was warmer than the last, but not enough to melt the snow where they were or, according to EOS, any other inland site in the United States.

Jonathan lifted off as soon as there was light, and began his trek. By about 10:00 a.m., he stopped to refuel at the Wendover cache. By noon, he was over what the GPS told him was Cheyenne Mountain, but all he saw was a mountain. However, northeast of the location, he could see bits of road and some partially buried structures that looked promising. He circled over the site, dropped a road flare, and was ready to fling the armed hand grenade down as hard as he could. Ken had calculated that it would be at least 250 feet and probably more like 400 feet below the plane when it went off, and unlikely to hit a gas tank.

Suddenly people were running out of one of the half-buried buildings, waving wildly. He came over them again and dropped the message and parachute. He watched it land, and then headed west to Utah to refuel.

Back in Eureka, Ken, Cathy, Jeanette, and Richard, one of Ken's students, were glued to the Volt's XM radio. The one weather report had ended about an hour ago, when suddenly the music stopped. An excited voice came on. "Wonderful news! An airplane just came over our site and dropped a message. We are running out to get the parachute that held it. There are other people still alive, and they have contacted us. There was no radio message of any kind, which puzzles us. But stay on this frequency. We will have more information any minute. All of the Cheyenne refugees are streaming up to the outside buildings. We may live after all. Wait, they are just coming in the door. The cylinder is being opened, and here is what it says:

Greetings to the Cheyenne Mountain refugees. We can hear your XM broadcasts, but have no way to respond. We are a small group of professors, scientists, and students from a West Coast university, committed to American democracy and Christian altruistic values, although all compatible beliefs, or none at all, are welcome. We will not tell you our location or the number of people in our party in case others with evil intent may hear and threaten us. However, we have repaired the plane you saw and can shuttle one person every four days from Cheyenne Mountain to our site well west of you, where the climate allows us to raise our own food. We request that you plan the exodus but meet our requirements. First, we will need a landing strip clear of snow. We would like 1,000 feet but we can do with a bit less. We will be very heavy taking off with people aboard. Second, do you have 91 octane lead-free gasoline? Without this, our rate of transfers is sharply reduced. Third, this plane is not able to handle storms or cold weather, so we have only about a month to make these transfers before winter. Thus, only a few of you can be transferred before the winter sets in. We will continue the transfers as soon as the weather allows in spring. We need you to give us weather reports, including the direction of the Yellowstone volcanic plume, before we can fly. Finally, our weight limits are extreme. We can take no one who weighs above 200 pounds, although perhaps we can go slightly above that in the future. We thus request that all transfers be intact young families, with the first being an M.D. with some light antibiotic medical supplies, followed by his or her spouse and children. We constantly monitor your frequency, and we have electrical power. Thus an amateur radio set should be an early transfer so that we can have two-way communications. We await your reply. Good luck to all of us, and God bless America!

"Whoever you are, you have given us hope where little hope had remained. We will get back to you with details after we all have a chance to analyze this message. Thank you for doing what appears to have been a dangerous rescue mission in an aircraft that, please accept my apologies, looks like it was made out of black plastic garbage bags. If that is so, and you have flown here in it, our admiration as members of the U.S. Air Force is without any limit. Thank you."

In the Eureka refuge, joy! Ken said, "Now we have contact, but we can't rest until Jonathan returns."

Many long, worrisome hours passed and the sun had just set

when they heard the airplane's engine. They directed the head-lights to light up the landing strip. After a nice landing, Jonathan collapsed in Jeanette's waiting arms. Ken and Cathy stood back, holding hands. All would be well this night.

14. FLIGHT FROM CHEYENNE MOUNTAIN

While there was joy and relief in the Eureka refuge about the successful contact with the Colorado refugees, the impact at Cheyenne Mountain was stunning. All sorts of fears and conflicts, which were starting to erode the social compact that had kept them sane in their snowy prison, were suddenly swept away.

That evening, the Eureka refugees heard a short XM communication.

This is lieutenant commander William Pierce, CEO of the Cheyenne Mountain Directorate. As you probably know, almost all NORAD work was moved out of this site in past years, and I was tasked to maintain the facility in a sort of mothballed configuration. Regretfully, some of the supplies originally stored for a long siege in the days of nuclear weapons were allowed to get old and spoiled, so that was when I was assigned in a matter of hours to

130

accept refugees, and support them for up to three years. I could find only enough rations for between 125 and 150 people. The triple blow of the tsunami waves (some of which were a mile high), the incredibly cold air, and the intense snowstorms did not affect us directly, but listening as all our contacts slowly perished one by one over that last year and a half was a soul-destroying trial. We had to assume we were alone, and when we attempted to exit through our main blast door, we were faced with a solid wall of snow. We eventually opened the door and left a four-foot crack through which we eventually tunneled to the surface, only to see a vast expanse of snow and no living creature. We set up an outside camp in some partially snow-covered buildings, and set up links especially to XM radio. I will use that link to communicate with you after the noon weather report each day. These reports will be brutally honest as we are entirely in your hands. Good night and thank you from the bottom of our hearts. We all will sleep well tonight, and tomorrow we will begin the tasks you outlined in your message.

Everybody always gathered at the Volt to hear the news from Cheyenne Mountain. The first reports told of the intense efforts by every man, woman, and child to clear a runway. There was a piece of road just northeast of their parking lot that had only a few feet of snow on it. Mass efforts with all shovels would be able to clear it. Probably within a week. A tunnel had been cut through the snow to the building that used to handle the federal carpool. It was under almost 40 feet of snow, but still they were able to reach the gasoline storage underground tanks. They were setting up pumps to extract the fuel, and estimated that it would take three days. Then there were comments about the fraying of the social compact as people were facing almost certain death in the near future. Despite the fact that they were a chosen group, many from the military, discipline problems were beginning to arise. All that ended instantly with the contact by the California angels, as the Eureka refugees were now called.

There were also some gratuitous comments:

"...Our engineers have analyzed pictures of your sailplane with motor, and we are stunned that it even flies. Do you know how many sacred tenets of aeronautical engineering you have violated? Our admiration for your initiative and courage knows no bounds. We also may have some materials that might help the plane. Your obvious lack of a radio comes to mind, and something to replace the black plastic that appears to be (but we hope it isn't) garbage bags. But there is not but one of us who would happily be in that plane regardless of risk factors."

Estimated completion of all tasks would be one week, and candidates for the first transfer were being vetted.

Ken asked his team for permission to fly to the Halcyon site, which the Arroyo Grande site was now being labeled in reference to an old religious community at the same site. Because two shipments of gasoline already had been sent down by boat, and the airstrip had been cleared weeks ago, Ken set off the next day. The now-familiar desolation of the Bay Area passed underneath, but off the coast of Monterey he could see what looked like whales in the ocean. On the land, not a trace of green was visible.

Arriving at Halcyon, he banked over the site and everybody dropped what they were doing and headed for the designated landing strip. Only the two-man boat crew, off the coast and normally housed in the ruins of Port San Luis up the coast a few miles, was absent.

As Ken climbed out of the plane on the short ladder pre-positioned at the airport, the first words he heard were, "Alice had her baby, and they are both perfect!" A strange feeling surged through Ken – hard to define, but powerful and moving. "They would survive, they would thrive, they would save the Earth."

Before leaving the airport, Ken refueled the airplane. By now, the boat crew was sailing right for the coast, because in the calm surf today beaching the boat was not difficult. Thus in about 40 minutes, the entire Halcyon team, with Andrew, Alice, and their baby, were seated in front of the main room of the colony, partially buried into the bank behind it. Ken luxuriated in the warmth, and saw how much had been done. Just down the slope, a substantial garden was growing, perhaps a half acre in extent, and to his left, he saw the chicken coop and a large pen. No trace of the willows planted within it remained.

It was all he could do to restrain himself as they all told of their successes, even about finding a leveled market in Arroyo Grande with some salvageable food in cans, and two gas stations that could be raided for fuel. Roger explained about the trials of getting steady irrigation water from a viable creek, and showed the bypass for the future waterwheel power source. Andrew proudly showed a string of fish just caught that morning, then he sat down next to Alice.

Ken could not resist. "How could you handle an additional 134 people by next summer?" he asked.

It took only seconds for them to reach the inevitable conclusion. "You have made contact!" Ken explained Jonathan's gutsy flight, and the quasi-delirious response of the Cheyenne Mountain refugees. He outlined plans at both ends, and finally mentioned that they requested the first transferee to be a young M.D. with some antibiotics.

The discussions that followed were positive and diverse, with everybody coming up with ways to support that many people. The clear conclusion was that at the earliest possible moment, probably enhanced by starting seeds in a cold frame, the acreage of the garden had to be made four times larger. The transferees, who would arrive one at a time, would gradually add to the available workforce.

"It would sure be nice to get electrical power to help build structures," said Jonathan.

"Done," said Ken. "Our creek will freeze within a month or two, and so I will disassemble all that I can and send the generators, pulleys, and bedpans down. That shipment will require both boats. We had better move soon because, the weather will deteriorate, at least up north."

Ken exchanged a few more words, all of which were positive, with the Halcyon meteorological team, and headed back to the airport. He had discovered on the return trip that flying inland was preferable as a means to avoid the northwest coastal winds. Even though that route was longer in time and distance, the flight consumed less fuel. Thus he was flying over the coastal mountains inland when below, south of the Clear Lake area, he spotted what looked like steam. Banking the plane, he saw to his amazement several acres of land clear of snow, and steam rising from vents. Considerable greenery was spread around, and perhaps even what appeared to be animals. "Phenomenal! The geysers! I should have known," Ken thought. "The geothermal area is exactly the kind of place that could provide shelter from the cold and melt the snow. I think the VW is about to make another cross-snow journey."

He landed just as the sun was setting, to the delight of the entire Eureka crew. Every arrival was special because they all knew the risks that Ken was taking in that rickety airplane.

"Alice has had her baby," he reported. "All is well at Halcyon, and I found new life and vegetation within 100 miles of here. How's that for a short but punchy report?" In return, Ken was happily punched by everyone present.

Ten days later, the report from Cheyenne Mountain was full of progress.

"With the help of every able-bodied person in Cheyenne Mountain, we have cleared a 1,000-foot landing area along the entrance road coming up the hill. That is the good news. The bad news is that the road is at a 6 percent grade, and has a slight curve in it. We have cut down all standing poles that might catch a wing on your approach. We have placed two large panels on the snow for your approach, one that says 300 feet and one that says 150 feet. If you are about at those heights, and then come in upslope, the landing should be possible if the winds are light. We have built a windsock at the very top of the landing strip to show the direction of the wind. Finally, if you are on the ground but about to roll off the edge, we have left 50 feet of loose snow to brake the plane, and then at the end some fluorescent orange fence webbing that will stop anything.

"We have more than 1,200 gallons of 91-octane fuel, if that is really what you need. We also have 100-octane aviation gas.

"Finally, we have a volunteer family for the first transfer. Navy surgeon Robert Wallace, M.D., 35 years old, 184 pounds, is our

first candidate. We also have another older doctor who can stay here. While Dr. Wallace's wife, Virginia, could come next, we would like to make a change and have their two young children, 6 and 9 years of age, come next, so that whatever happens, they have at least one parent. The combined weight of the children is 145 pounds, so that might allow for the radio you requested. Finally, Virginia Wallace, 138 pounds, comes last. She is a registered nurse, but has not been practicing recently.

"We see a window from September 25 through September 28 as the best time for the first transfer. We will be ready here on those three days."

September 25 broke clear and cool, with low winds. Ken and Jonathan were out before dawn, adding below the pilot's seat a small container that held seven additional gallons of gas for dire emergencies. It would have to be hand-pumped to get to the main tanks. The plan was to fly at about 150 mph, at about the highest comfortable altitude that would get Jonathan to Cheyenne Mountain about noon. Time for refueling, pick up the passenger, and then head for Wendover to refuel, then maybe Golconda Summit to refuel, depending on fuel use with the heavy load, and finally to Eureka, arriving rather late. Landing might have to be accomplished by car headlights.

The flight to Colorado was flawless, although Jonathan could see the Yellowstone ash plume on the northern horizon as he approached Cheyenne Mountain, now for the second time. The markings were easy to see, and he throttled back and began the approach. He had no way to judge how high he was over the markers, but the cleared black road was easy to see. He throttled back more and at the last minute pulled the nose up for a perfect landing about halfway up the runway. He gunned the engine to reach the top, then used the rudder to swing the plane 180 degrees as he cut the engine.

Suddenly he realized something they had forgotten. He needed a ladder to climb out. He opened the canopy, patched as it was in a dozen places, and said, "Hi, there. I need a ladder to get down." He was ticked because his lack of foresight might take away from his spectacular landing. No problem, there. The Air Force and Navy pilots were in awe as they rushed up to the plane. "My God, it *is* trash bags!" one said, as Jonathan climbed down on the hood of the Jeep used to help clear the landing strip that had been quickly driven up to the plane with the needed fuel in the back.

Time was short, so as Jonathan told them how to fill the tanks, Robert Wallace came up. As they shook hands, Jonathan checked Robert's clothes to make sure he would be warm enough. Virginia was trying to be strong, but the two kids were clinging to his legs. Commander Pierce came up as the pilots were going over every inch of the plane, amazed it could hold together with the strain of the propeller way too far back for even minimum stability. Com mander Pierce said, "Son, you should get the Presidential Medal of Honor for even flying this contraption, and the landing was a work of art."

Jonathan replied, "From you guys, that is the highest compliment I could imagine. Let's save the cheering for when I get Robert back to safety."

It was only about 20 minutes later when Robert was crammed into the forward cargo compartment. They had replaced some of the trash bags with transparent plastic so he could see left and right, but not forward. The engine fired up nicely on the 91-octane fuel.

"That engine was never designed to work with that octane," one pilot mentioned to his friend. "How did they do that?"

The loaded airplane was heavy, and used about two-thirds of the runway, but lifted nicely and turned to the west.

XM radio had been reporting the entire landing as it happened, and the California teams could hear the cheer as the plane lifted off.

They landed west of Wendover, where the plane taxied and stopped alongside a small ladder. Robert, who asked to be called Bob, climbed out gratefully to stretch his cramped legs, and helped refuel. Jonathan was pleased to see that they were significantly under the fuel use estimates despite the extra weight. "I think we can make Eureka in one hop," said Jonathan. "So that is where we are going?" asked Bob. "We had no idea."

After refueling was completed, they climbed back into the airplane, and then needed a longer run to take off because they didn't have the slope that helped at Cheyenne Mountain. Wendover had almost a mile of wind-cleared roadway, so they had no problem with takeoff.

It was in the last bit of sunlight when Ken heard the engine, and the Gossamer Phoenix came in for a landing. As Jonathan climbed out, he said, "Almost had to use my emergency reserve, because we had some headwinds for the last 200 miles."

Bob extracted himself from the nose, and stepped down, and said. "This is it?" The airport was of course almost empty, with one shed. But the Jeep and the Volt were both there to take everybody back to the refuge. As they approached and stopped, Bob looked out, stunned. All around was a wasteland, with not a shred of green. All he could see was sand and some debris piles. The look on his face said it all. Ken chimed in, "It's home. You'll get to appreciate it." Bob asked, "How many of you are there?" Ken responded, "Up here, we have six people, now seven with you. At our southern site, we have eight people, plus a new baby. After you check out our people for health, we will send you south in a boat to Halcyon, where it is warmer and where most of your people will end up. But this pile of debris is part of a ruined hospital, and it saved our lives in the first year's severe cold."

As Bob walked in, he could now see greenhouses, and felt the heat of the fire. Climbing into the building, he could see signs of careful organization superimposed on what looked like hospital basement storage rooms. Finally, in Room 4, the fire was burning cheerfully, and there were fluorescent lights, and chairs in a kitchen area. He sat down impressed.

Then he said, "Your whole group consists of only 14 people and a baby, yet you are optimistically planning to rescue 134 people?"

Ken replied grimly, "Do you have any idea how few people still live in this world? The tsunami, intense and prolonged cold, and the great snows have decimated the Northern Hemisphere, and we expect the Southern Hemisphere may be worse, because that was where the impact occurred. We believe that the current cold condition, which may slightly ameliorate as the volcanoes simmer down, is the new standard. We are in an ice age!"

Jonathan wanted to go back the next day, but Ken forced him to sleep, eat, and relax a bit while they made some repairs to the airplane and refueled it.

Thus it was September 27 when Jonathan lifted off in the first frail light of morning. Again a good flight, another good landing at Cheyenne Mountain, but slightly skewed by a crosswind. A ladder was ready for him this time, and a whole crew began to refuel the plane. They even checked the main tire pressure.

Virginia walked up with two children all bundled up. Her eyes were red, but her determination to save her children was steel. Commander Pierce said, "Having measured your cargo space, we have built a frame that allows the children to sit tandem with the top one not squashing to bottom. We also ask permission to include their pet cat, in a suitable cage. Both children have been taught how to use the urine collection system. We have given them both headphones that we can run to this module that we can attach beside you using duct tape," Pierce said, almost cringing at the word. "It has their favorite music, but by speaking into this mike you can talk to them and they can respond. They have been mildly sedated."

"Nicely done," said Jonathan. "Load up and on we go." He walked over and gave Virginia a big hug. She broke down into tears, carefully facing away so her children could not see. "I will take good care of them, and their father awaits them anxiously. You will all be together in a week with warm winds, the ocean, and some green plants in a loving community." She sniffed, squeezed his hand, and backed away to wave cheerily at the children. They, however, looked like zombies. "Industrial-strength sedative," thought Jonathan.

Finally, a radio was placed all the way forward in the cargo area, well away from the children's feet. Jonathan asked, "Do you have two of those? We have two locations for our colony." Commander Pierce snapped his fingers and a tech ran off. "Actually, no, this was the one we were to use. But we can make another in a day. By the way, all transmissions are encoded. Nobody else can read the signal. I gather you had some trouble?"

"Yes. It was resolved, but it cost us one of our refugees. We had an encounter with members of the Zetas Mexican drug cartel, all heavily armed," Jonathan said.

The tech ran up, with a few wires dangling. Jonathan asked carefully, "Do you have any waterproof trash bags? I would hate to have these get wet with a salty fluid that we'll likely have on board."

Pierce almost cracked up laughing – he hadn't laughed in two years – and came back with something far better, a plastic water-proof pouch that could hold both radios.

The takeoff was a bit iffy with the crosswind, and the plane yawed badly just after liftoff, but Jonathan corrected quickly and gave the engine more power. "There goes my perfect record," mused Jonathan. He refueled at Golconda Summit, which was harder all by himself and required almost 30 minutes, but then he took off to the west, noting that the Mt. Shasta plume was almost gone. He landed a little earlier than the last time because of milder headwinds, but didn't like the look of the western sky. The landing was fine, and Bob Wallace ran up to the airplane. With tender hands, he extracted the kids and their cat. With the plane safely secured in the makeshift wooden hangar, everyone went back to the refuge for a happy reunion. The kids were still a bit groggy. Jonathan said, "They told me they were sedated, but whatever they used must have been industrial strength."

It was a late but happy dinner. The kids were fed and were soon asleep in the dormitory, with their father's bed next to theirs. The cat was curled up on the blankets. Ken mused, "Now maybe we can use some of the cat food we found for a real cat."

Ken was not great with radios, but the instructions were pretty clear. He strung a rhombic antenna over the debris field with a favored direction to Cheyenne Mountain. He turned it on. Nothing. In fact, it was only the next day when it suddenly came to life. It had taken Cheyenne Mountain two days to build another radio. Ken responded immediately. "Tell Virginia all is well – kids, dad, and cat. Would she like to talk to them?"

"Oh, yes!" came the reply.

The repairs and improvements on the boat named Paul were just being completed, and it was about ready to go. The next day the rains came, and for three days they were all confined to the refuge. Bob had done a complete health check of everyone with the limited tools he had at his disposal, and found that they were in splendid shape. "I wish the people in Cheyenne Mountain would be this fit," he mentioned. By now Jeanette was showing her pregnancy. She was due in about two months. Ken wanted to get her south as soon as possible.

Ken said, "Bob, when we get Virginia, we will fly her directly to Halcyon. I hope that will be in a few days, pending information from Cheyenne Mountain. These plastics get brittle when cold, and if a rip started, it could bring down the plane. We have double layers to prevent that, but I don't expect we can fly much more this year."

Bob asked, "Can we take four adults and two kids south?"

"Piece of cake," responded Ken. "The seas are good, the winds fresh, and our sailing skills are by now well–honed."

So Bob, his two kids, and Jeanette set off for Halcyon on September 30, since the seas had calmed down. The second ham radio transceiver was safely placed in the Cheyenne Mountain waterproof sack and sent south with them. Soon the groups would be able to talk to one another. The ride south to Halcyon was generally an easy and fast trip because of steady northwest winds.

It wasn't until October 6 that Cheyenne Mountain gave the OK to fly in. Again, Jonathan made the hop without refueling, but they still had 40 gallons at both Wendover and Golconda Summit. The plane had needed more than the usual repairs after the trip. Some of the plastic was breaking down in the cold and constant wind shear. "We have to do better," thought Ken. "Even having double bags to mitigate damage if the outer layers tear is still too scary."

Virginia almost leaped into the plane as soon as it was refueled. The takeoff was excellent, but the headwinds from the north were strong. They had to go south to avoid some Yellowstone plume, but it was smaller than it had been a month ago. They landed west of Wendover and topped off with all the fuel there. Jonathan noted his fuel use and the northern winds. He was planning to go south to Halcyon and the wind would actually help that. He took off and headed southwest, regularly checking his fuel use. When he was south of Golconda Summit, he was pleased to see that he was doing better than he had planned.

Every time the airplane landed at Halcyon, everyone streamed over to welcome them. The plane rolled to a stop and Bob brought the ladder with his two kids in tow. "Momma," they screamed, as Virginia unwound herself from the cramped cargo space. Jeanette smiled, for she would soon be a momma, too, and she was especially pleased that a doctor and nurse would be there to help her.

Cheyenne Mountain predicted that one more two-day calm

period would occur after October 20, and the air would be un-seasonably warm. After some discussion, a single person would be chosen to make what would be the last trip of the year. Regret-fully, there were no experts on agriculture at Cheyenne Mountain, so a young technician was chosen to provide technical support at Eureka, which missed the talents of Roger now that he was committed to Halcyon. A 27-year-old Air Force technician named Johan Akselsson, a Minnesota Swede who knew something about cold air conditions, was chosen. The flight was about as good as it could get, but winds forced Jonathan to use up the last of the Golconda Summit fuel. Upon arrival at Eureka, they placed the airplane in the hangar and the group made a concerted effort to protect it over the winter.

15. THE COLD: YEAR 3

The biggest change for the third winter was that they were all in daily contact with each other by the security-encoded short-wave radio link. That communication enormously alleviated the sense of loneliness of the previous winters, especially during the periods of intense cold.

Cheyenne Mountain continued the XM uplink broadcasts, but then added a series of popular amateur radio bands that they would constantly scan. The XM broadcasts included general information about the evacuation of Cheyenne Mountain without identifying specific places and people. They were still stunned that the California refugees numbered only 14, and that most of them were students. They had done so much, in addition to being well on the way to saving their lives.

At the Eureka refuge

One week later after the last flight, the first hard freeze occurred, but it was a relatively toasty 89 below zero F, with a high of 20 below. It lasted for five full days. Still somehow this cold was discouraging because it showed that any improvement would happen slowly. Everyone was getting tired of being trapped inside for parts of the winter.

In the periods when it was warm enough, Johan joined Ken, David, and the crew in getting ready for two events. One would be the resumption of the Cheyenne Mountain flights, and the other was accessing the bare soil green area Ken saw over the geysers, north of Santa Rosa. Because no landing was possible anywhere near the site, the best approach would be to try to make the Jeep into a four-wheel drive snow machine, something the VW couldn't do. Also, the Cherokee had ample space for collected samples, which could prove useful. Finally, with a three-person team and the winch, much longer trips could be attempted.

The plan was to wait until the first cold spring rains had fallen on the new snow, which froze at night. The overnight freeze created a very sturdy crust that could support a lot of weight. The paddles pointing outward would be attached to the wheels, resulting in a contact area six times the size of the tire surface. The addition of the paddles also made the Jeep much wider and harder to turn. Still, it was a project that could go on when the weather wasn't too atrocious. Regretfully, without the electric systems so generously shipped down to Halcyon, the work was slow. All holes in the wheels had to be drilled by hand.

Still, having not one but two critical projects meant that the wintertime blues were minimal. They had plenty of food, lots of smoked salmon, a few eggs each day, and the remains of the frozen cooked meat that were stored in the bedpans in the refrigerator. Johan simply did not know how to respond when he saw the first meat brought out. He didn't know whether to laugh or cringe. But he hesitated only a short time, and found that the meat was still good, though a bit dry. They had abundant salmon, but began to find the limited diet boring. The hope was that the blackberry vines, safely protected in the greenhouse in time of intense cold, would give them some sweet preserves next year. They had been growing like weeds, although now they were dormant in winter.

At Halcyon

Halcyon was in fine form, with Bob's family and medical expertise most welcome. The big news was the birth of Jonathan and Jeanette's baby in early December, in what might almost appear a real hospital as long as you didn't look too hard. There were now several partially dug-in dwellings along the southwest sloping bank. Each had a refuge room in the very back that could be sealed off, and a small wood stove for heating, with a small chimney through the dirt to the air – high enough to protect it from being covered by snow. Food and water were cached for a few days. They still had not yet gone through one winter there, and they feared the cold.

Roger's purloined power system was working pretty well, but the nature of the stream made harnessing its power more difficult than in Eureka. Roger and his constant team of students continually modified trenches and spillways to get more reliable and abundant power. Regretfully, for all their scavenging, they found only two working fluorescent 60-watt light bulbs, but planned to ask for some of the hospital fixtures from Eureka next spring. The prime use of the power was for the daily radio contact.

The winter was heralded not by cold or snow but by powerful Pacific storms. The "Good Ship Peter," as it was now called, was tied up at Port San Luis when the weather was passable. The weather was never good so they always stayed close to shore while fishing, and they hauled it out of the water with a trolley when things looked too grim. They built a shelter near the boat for the crew if they got trapped when the cold came, because they were several miles away from Halcyon. The fishing continued to be very good, and it was the main source of protein.

Everyone except the boat crew pitched in during the harvest. Bob and Virginia's kids delighted in harvesting snow peas; however, they ate a fair fraction themselves. Nobody minded too much, but they were disappointed that their hoped-for seed production from some species such as cabbage had not occurred. They decided to start more plants in cold frames to extend the growing season. Still, they had a pretty diverse diet, rich in snow peas and potatoes. Bob was actually pleased with the diet. He said, "It's almost like the South Beach Diet if you ignore the potatoes, and it's better than what we ate at Cheyenne Mountain."

By Christmas, they experienced only one light snow, and while the temperature got down to zero, the really bitter cold snap they feared had not occurred. Many trees could survive such conditions if it didn't get much worse. Roger's survey teams were pleased that they had found no permafrost.

At Cheyenne Mountain

By now, the Cheyenne Mountain contingent knew exactly how few people were involved in trying to rescue them, and they were not about to be shown up by these genius California heroes. A new urgency and spirit surged through Cheyenne Mountain. The bitter cold descended on them as before, but they extended their tunnels under the snow well into the machine shop and carpool areas in the parking lot southwest of the main entrance.

Two years earlier, just before they had closed Cheyenne Mountain as the first "Siberian cold" descended, a last group of four refugees and a pilot had flown in and sort of landed on the parking lot. The plane, a Piper Seneca V, was towed into the carpool main garage, right up against the retaining wall. It was gasoline from this plane that they had offered Jonathan on the first landing.

The collapse of the garage roof under the snow totally flattened the forward part of the garage near the parking lot, but against the retaining wall the roof had held, making a triangular-shaped cave. When they penetrated the area this time, they found that the Piper's nose at the wall was undamaged, but the tail structure had been flattened by the roof collapse. Having seen for himself the California aircraft and knowing how fragile and risky it was, Commander Pierce realized that the Seneca V, with a range about 800 miles, might be able to reach the coast of California and carry a few people at a time. The key point was that they now knew exactly where they could go to get out of the snow and cold. Until they were contacted by the California group, they had no idea what was out there, and they were in despair.

They had to stop work for a few days around Christmas because a severe cold snap pushed temperatures down to 148 degrees below zero, and even the protected tunnels became too cold. Christmas was festive in a way that had not happened in the past two years, with even a small bit of smoked salmon Jonathan had brought them on his third flight.

The Air Force and Navy pilots, with their wives and kids, went to work. At the widest part of the garage-snow cave, they built a stove that produced some heat. Even so, the work had to stop for a few days. They took the wings off the plane and one team brought the front section out of the cave into a temporary structure where they could test the engines. The aircraft was designed for 100-octane fuel, but they had almost none of that. What they had was an abundant supply of 91-octane gasoline, which was formulated for cars. A quick radio contact to California confirmed that they had not yet found any aviation fuel in the small airports they had checked. Immediately, the engineers went to work to modify the two aircraft engines for 91-octane gas with the help of some pointers from Ken and Roger about how they had done the conversion.

Although the airplane's tail had been crushed, Cheyenne Mountain still had a good machine shop and abundant power from a small nuclear reactor, and reconstructing the flattened tail took only a week. By mid-February, they knew they would have a working aircraft by March. They estimated that the 91-octane fuel would reduce the range to perhaps 650 to 700 miles, so they converted the back cargo area into an extra gas tank, allowing them to fly an estimated 1,000 miles.

This news was received with unmitigated joy, especially by Ken and Jonathan who better than anyone else knew how hard it was going to be to empty Cheyenne Mountain using their powered sailplane. The Cheyenne Mountain group also had found rolls of thin Mylar, and volunteered to re-skin the plane without using garbage bags. They breathed vast sighs of relief in Eureka, because a rip in the garbage bag would have resulted in a quick death to plane and passengers, and the loss of almost all life in Cheyenne Mountain. In Eureka, work on the plane essentially ceased once it was flyable, as they awaited delivery of the much stronger Mylar.

16. SPRING: YEAR 3

At Eureka

Spring was late coming to Eureka, confirming Ken's pessimism about any rapid warmup of the Earth. But by April, the abundant snows were interspersed with cold rain and at night it all froze. The area around the refuge was now clear of snow, which meant mud. Travel off the roads was virtually impossible.

Ken, Johan, and David would be the main explorers, while Lisa, one of Ken's students, followed in the VW. Only Rachel, a physics student, who was really becoming Eureka's gardener, would stay behind to guard the refuge, and feed the chickens. Everyone, including Lisa and Rachel, was well armed. They would all drive the roads as far as they could until they reached snow, and then the VW would return to the refuge while the Jeep moved on. The key thing was that Ken's photos did not show enough to ascertain whether the big Eel River Bridge at Fortuna had survived. Twenty miles later, they were still driving on the road, often over sand and mud layers, but still over pavement. When they got to the bridge, the reason for the confusion in the photos was evident. One span had fallen at the bank end, which was undercut, but the rest was intact. The river was still low because not much rain had fallen, and the snow at its sources did not melt. They were able to drive down the bank and onto the partially downed span. At that point, Lisa turned back and the Jeep pressed on.

About 10 miles farther, snow on the road increased, and they reached the point at which it was completely covered with snow. This was also about the inland limit of the tsunami, and beyond, the redwood forest stood straight and tall, and very dead. Most branches had fallen off, but the roots were anchored in permafrost, so few had fallen over. An enormous forest of giant telephone poles anchored in snow appeared as far as they could see up the valley. It was a bizarre sight.

They switched to the snow paddles, which they had never really tried in any extensive way, but the Jeep rode high over the snow – its undercarriage toboggan not even touching the snow. Soon they were travelling at about 30 miles per hour, with David leaning out the window and constantly checking on the paddles. So far, so good. In fact, except for some modest detours, the route was passable all the way to the region where they climbed out of redwood country. Here the snow was even deeper, bridging whole streams. The going, if anything, became easier. As the sun was setting, they reached an area where the town of Willits should have been. The snow was so deep that nothing was visible but the dead tops of oaks.

"Somewhere under that snow is the grave of the famous race-horse Seabiscuit, which survived enormous odds to race and win after a bad accident," mused Ken. "He should be our mascot in spirit."

They stopped the Jeep next to a dead oak tree, broke off branches, and started a fire. The air temperature was below freezing but not bitter, and they were both excited and content.

The next morning the sun was bright and clear, and they started out for Asti, where the road took off for the geysers. There were essentially no road markers to go by, but Ken's Garmin GPS could give them directions and recalculated them when they drifted off the road and into the snow. Eventually a valley appeared and, against the sky, steam. They were by now going across country and turned off the Garmin's female voice, which was having a fit. The terrain was steep, but they worked their way to the bottom of the valley, being careful to avoid breaking through to an unseen stream below, kept flowing by the warm water. Finally, around a hillock, they saw a large steam plume, and below it, bare ground and plants. Lots of plants!

They brought the Jeep as close as they dared. The roaring steam made conversation difficult. But on inspection, there were lots of steam vents and water pools. They carefully moved onto the bare ground that appeared firm and a bit away from the big steam vent to check out the plants. There were plants growing in the warm water running down in rivulets, but outside of that, there was a large field of what looked like very ordinary grass. Ken hauled out his camera and went wild with pictures. By now, all three refuges had laptop computers and flash drives, so when travel became available in a few weeks, they could share the photos.

The field appeared to have been grazed low to the ground.

All in all, several hundred acres were free of snow and mostly vegetated, including what looked like a bushy oak tree. Its top had been repeatedly killed, probably by the cold, but the warmed roots kept sprouting. Its leaves, too, had been grazed to about six feet above the ground. Finally, dropping down toward the creek, they saw an entire flock of sheep. How they had gotten there was beyond comprehension, but the fact that they, rather than goats, survived was probably due to their fleece and the warmed oasis. There they were, perhaps three dozen in all.

Somehow the sight of terrestrial animals was an emotional closure for all of them. "We would have animal companions after all," Ken thought. He wanted to run up and hug one, but they looked pretty wild. The opportunity would come later, after the refugees had grazing lands ready for them.

They spent the next three hours collecting all the types of vegetation that they thought might possibly survive outside the geysers. The grass in the runoff water and some reeds actually growing in steaming water they ignored, but they carefully cut away three parts of two oak tree bushes, lots of plugs of grass, and a bush that looked like *Ceanothus americanus* – New Jersey tea – and packed them into the Jeep. Finally, Ken picked a featureless part of the area and dug into the ground, collecting everything and soil into a black trash bag. It took Ken and David together to get it into the Jeep.

The return trip was of necessity slow, although they all wanted to race home. Their tracks from the approach were an excellent guide. They camped once again under the same tree near Willits, and ran the engine twice at night to keep the plants warm. They didn't have much gas to spare.

The next day, they were crossing the Fortuna Bridge on the Eel River when they spotted Lisa in the VW. "I had estimated that you might possibly be here today, but you have done great," she said. "You have no idea," replied Ken, and they began to show off their treasures. "And we found sheep," said Ken.

"You have got to be kidding! How could they survive?" Lisa asked.

"Well, how did we survive?" asked Ken. "We found warmth, food, and water. The geysers have all three, and the sheep have thick coats."

At Halcyon

Roger's meteorological team had analyzed the area and concluded that in the first awful winter, the severe cold had penetrated the area and frozen the ground, killing any plants that had survived the tsunami. The ground was as sterile as near Eureka, but by now it had no permafrost below an elevation of about 1,000 feet.

The Halcyon refugees could barely wait for spring, especially since the winter had never gotten too bad. But about the time they had hoped to start planting, a never-ending string of rainstorms came through – all causing massive erosion and washing out the intake to the waterwheel. Cold, wet, and dark, they toughed out six weeks until May, when the storms abated and the sun appeared. Their foresight was well rewarded, because in the cold frames the seeds were well started and could in many cases be planted directly into the wet ground where seeds would have rotted. The amount of hand labor to plant was enormous, but they had 13 people now and all helped, all day. In about 10 days, thousands of plants were in the ground, even corn plants. They were rewarded by warm weather and increasing sunshine, which actually felt warm.

They repaired the waterwheel, and the Good Ship Peter was now regularly at sea, fishing and collecting kelp. The chickens were expanding in number and eating mostly kelp and willow shoots, enhanced by garbage, and their eggs were most welcome.

Jeanette had cultured the last two redwood burls, which had sprouted nicely. They were still in pots but the estimates were that they could survive in the climate. Roger had started his own meteorological team the prior summer, and they by now had a good record of eight months of weather conditions. By checking other records stored in Ken's laptop, they saw that the climate approximated what southern Oregon and Northern California had known prior to the impact.

The green swatches down along the Santa Maria River proved to be the same plants seen at Arroyo Grande Creek, but they were expanding their range all by themselves. The refugees found more food at wrecked markets, and they were now ranging as far north as the old Pismo Beach.

Clearly, Halcyon had passed a key threshold and was now self-sufficient, but could it support 134 people? Not currently, was the estimate. But Halcyon would do its best, because it was the best site found to date.

At Cheyenne Mountain

There was no discernable spring at Cheyenne Mountain. It was always cold, but not as extreme as the brutal "great colds," as they called them. On April 1, they broadcast the entire day on XM radio an analysis of climate trends. The slow recovery from the cold was now beyond doubt, as was the fact that large parts of the United States would remain snow-covered for eight to 15 years, with the exception of parts of Florida and the Gulf Coast east of New Orleans in the coastal regions.

The good news was that the band of heavy clouds seen by a weather satellite was starting to thin and shred, with clear parts now seen in northern Mexico. The computer models indicated that the cooling ocean was decreasing the intensity of the equatorial storms and the tropical jet stream. As more sunlight reached the Earth's surface, warming accelerated. Some cloud thinning also was taking place in the far Southern Hemisphere, at the lower tip of South America in southern Patagonia. The view into Antarctica was still hazy, probably from sulfates.

The vastly enhanced stratospheric sulfuric acid cloud was also slowly being stripped out of the sky. The people of Cheyenne Mountain had set up a meteorological site above their refuge in the summer of year two. While it had to be abandoned during the great colds, it was now getting good information, including the orange color of the sunsets caused by the pollution.

However, it was late May before the temperatures relented enough so that they could once again clear the runway – this time for the Seneca V, which needed more takeoff space than the California powered sailplane. Refugees at Halcyon were actively pumping gas from abandoned filling stations and transporting it down to the airport. They built a shed to house these supplies, and grandiosely painted a sign that said, "Halcyon International Airport."

Ken and Roger's food team transplanted a selection of the plants collected from the geysers area. They planted grass plugs in about 12 sites with the best sun exposure, right next to the growing willow hedge near the creek. Eventually it would be a pasture for the sheep from the geysers, but it would take at least a couple of years before they could bring as many as six sheep to the new pasture. They planted three oak trees slightly above them on the bank with good drainage. Finally, they planted a wide row of *Ceanothus americanus* bushes just behind the row of earth-shelter homes, now expanded greatly and extended to a second set higher on the bank. Every family would have one home, but many single males and females were living in two separate dormitories at Cheyenne Mountain.

The pilots at Cheyenne Mountain were not yet ready to fly because they were still digging out their airport, so Ken started a series of exploration flights covering the area. However, he was more nervous than before, knowing the airplane's vulnerability to wind and storms, and was anxious to still be alive when the Mylar finally arrived. He became more conservative in his fuel estimates. Jonathan could have made these flights perfectly well, but now he was a family man.

The persistent cloud deck had shifted south by about 50 miles, so that the Santa Barbara area and the Channel Islands were now in the clear. Ken's reconnaissance flights were discouraging, because the wreckage of Santa Barbara was as complete as any other West Coast site. Ken wondered whether the severe cold might have been tempered passing over the ocean to Santa Rosa Island, just across the sound from Santa Barbara. As he approached the island's north coast, he saw nothing. But as he passed over the ridge, he saw a distinct belt of vegetation down by the water on the south coast. Not just a little – a wide band. He took pictures and swept low. The vegetation was in the form of green shoots, several feet high, and they appeared to be growing out of stumps that had been sheared off at the base. "Eucalyptus, I bet," he thought to himself. "The ultimate survivor has survived!"

Returning to the airstrip, Ken landed and gave his report that evening, complete with a slide show on his laptop, now that Roger's team had the waterwheel power station on line. "Good news and bad news," Ken said while showing the pictures. "Eucalyptus, which was supposed to be removed from Santa Rosa Island as an invasive species, survived, sprouting from roots. The stuff is not much good for anything but inferior lumber, but beggars can't be choosers. We are going to have forests again."

Since the Good Ship Peter had earlier returned to Eureka, Ken radioed a request to load it with more smoked salmon, head south and prepare it for an expedition to Santa Rosa Island. In three days, the entire two-boat flotilla and a skiff manufactured during the winter at Port San Luis were ready, awaiting the weather report from Cheyenne Mountain.

About a week later, people at Cheyenne Mountain gave the OK. No major storms were boiling up from the tropics, a high-pressure ridge was in place, and the winds were moderate from the west, easing travel both down and back.

Five days later, the two ships returned, each with three Eucalyptus saplings with roots balled in burlap. Andrew was not sanguine about whether they could all survive because they had to cut a lot of root. But they planted the saplings in what they now called "The Halcyon National Forest," complemented by tubs holding the two redwood shoots.

17. FLIGHT OF THE WILD GEESE

About one week later, time had come for the first test flight of the Seneca V. The event was broadcast live over XM satellite radio. The worst part was manhandling the plane across the snow to the cleared area. Because of the longer runway needed, the road had been cleared to about 1,500 feet, but the slope was a steady 7 percent at the base. Takeoff downhill would be easy, but it would be a tricky landing. Still, Jonathan had done it in the trash bag sailplane contraption, so the best pilots in the western United States' Air Force and Navy all wanted to be the first. Most of them, however, hadn't flown a propeller-driven plane in years. Finally, three with recent propeller experience in trainers were chosen, and they used a lottery to determine the pilots' order of flights. They would rotate for each additional flight, including three test flights, before attempting the trip to Halcyon.

Navy lieutenant Benjamin Halsey, grandson of the famous Bill Halsey of World War II fame, won the lottery. In retrospect, it was easy. The plane was light and needed less than 1,000 feet to take off. Ben then flew over and around the area, going miles in each direction, before coming back to land. He did exactly as Jonathan had done – he came in very low, nose up, and almost stalled the airplane. Flawless!

When he climbed out to boisterous cheers, he did not have the look of satisfaction and joy that everyone expected. "It is awful out there. Colorado Springs is almost buried in snow above the roofs of most buildings. It's as though we are at the South Pole Station in Antarctica." His own house, of course, had been down there.

They made two flights per day, with increasing weight on board, until all three pilots were comfortable with the plane. They then had a detailed discussion over the radio about whether or not Cheyenne Mountain should be abandoned. Ken took the position that there was an awful lot of irreplaceable high technology up there, including satellite interception capabilities for weather, and that with most people removed, the existing food would be enough for decades. Personnel could be rotating in and out from California, and food could be enhanced by shipments from the West Coast. Commander Pierce strongly seconded this suggestion, but the next problem to be faced was the decision about who among them would be willing to stay behind.

With amazing alacrity, two sergeants – one male and one female – and a technician volunteered to stay. "Will that be enough?" asked Roger. "Oh, yes," said Pierce. "This place is almost entirely on autopilot. For amusement, we have almost every film ever made in our libraries, and these three have their own reasons for staying here."

Ken was amazed, but said nothing. Bob, seeing his eyebrows inflect, said, "Best not to inquire too closely on that. It was a sign of the collapse of conventional moral strictures as the despair set in. They will keep themselves amused, I assure you."

Through the radio, Pierce authoritatively stated, "We have 126 people to transfer. We can take only three at a time in the Seneca V, because of the extra fuel we must carry. We are allowing no more than 30 pounds of clothes, books, and supplies per person. Later we can make some cargo flights and take more, so each person can have two piles, immediate and potentially future, the latter being 50 pounds. I understand that you are short on clothing, according to Bob."

Ken piped up, "It is amazing what you can do with an unlimited supply of hospital gowns if you don't mind everybody's butt showing."

"So I hear," said Pierce.

Starting June 20, shuttle flights were made every day, with pilots at both Halcyon and Cheyenne Mountain alternating. With two gaps to avoid bad weather and three to keep away from the still-potent Yellowstone ash and sulfur plume, by mid-August almost all people scheduled to leave Cheyenne Mountain were out.

Most were delivered at Halcyon, but two groups were sent to Eureka at their choice, because there was much to do there. One was the senior M.D., who was itching to excavate the hospital and see what could be salvaged. With him was his young, attractive medical technician, Maria Gonzalez. She had endured three years of essentially constant propositions in Cheyenne Mountain, but her strong Catholic faith and the nature of the sleaze mongers making the advances helped her to resist advances and survive intact.

David had assumed more and more of the leadership of the Eureka refuge, and was being trained as a sailplane pilot, since Jonathan preferred to stay in Halcyon with his growing family. One of Ken's original agnostics, David, had converted to Christianity and had been baptized by Father John about a year ago. Maria and David immediately hit it off. Within weeks, they were both talking to John about marriage.

The last flight was to contain critical cargo and only one passenger, all destined for Halcyon.

For the occasion, the entire population of Halcyon was lining the runaway. They set up a table with a buffet that was rich in fish dishes but also included some of the last meat flown down from Eureka in the Gossamer Phoenix, which was looking resplendent in its semi-transparent Mylar sheathing.

There was even a small band, formed by some of the people from Cheyenne Mountain who had brought their musical instruments.

Finally, at nearly sunset, they heard the Seneca's engine in the distance.

The Seneca came in neatly on the strip, and taxied up to the waiting crowd. A single figure stepped out, tall and white haired. When he saw the crowd, his face broke into that familiar grin rarely used in the past three years. His wife ran up and hugged him, and two kids wrapped their arms around his legs.

Ken stepped forward, "Welcome to California, Mr. President."

18. RENAISSANCE

As the refugees had arrived from Cheyenne Mountain throughout the summer, they had been added to existing teams mostly in accord with their desires. Many were so entranced by seeing growing plants again that they volunteered for the farm fields. The first lady took over one of the teams focusing on vegetables. Several Navy people joined the Port San Luis team and immediately started talking about building a much larger, oceangoing sailboat.

The Air Force people were all over the local airports, with teams searching out fuel from ruined airports and trying to salvage anything they could. Roger had gained a lot of technical people who were in the process of increasing the electric power by various means available, including a windmill.

The machine shop was now the second largest structure in Halcyon after the main conference and dining area, and had benefited from transfers of hardware that the Seneca's weight limits enabled to be carried from Cheyenne Mountain. One immediate gain was two-way radios that were issued to everyone who left Halcyon to Eureka on exploration trips so they could be in constant contact with the base and Cheyenne Mountain.

After the arrival of the last transfers from Cheyenne Mountain, a meeting of all of the survivors was called for the next Sunday, after John had finished conducting Mass at Halcyon. People from Eureka and Cheyenne Mountain listened with their radios. It was time to address the organization of this much larger group. They had worked well and cooperatively with each other so far, but perhaps something more formal was required. Ken suggested the format of the New England town hall meeting, in which every voter in a town could be together to decide important matters. The referendum would then be implemented by a small group of elected selectmen and the town staff.

Because the population of all three sites totaled only 148 people, excluding the babies, that was a workable solution. The president remained extremely low key but entirely supportive. His comment was that the United States in which he was elected to serve no longer existed, and he would do anything he could to form a new government, as along as it adhered to the highest and best values of the U.S. Constitution and Christian charity.

The meeting was amazingly smooth. All the Cheyenne Mountain people had learned the incredible risk that the California "angels" had taken to save them, and freely admitted the gift of their lives. The ad hoc team arrangements were slightly shifted, but still had the three major foci: 1) climate, ecology, and food; 2) technology, exploration, and infrastructure; and 3) social, medical, and educational needs. A formal Navy and Air Force were designated, although the personnel could and would be moved around as the needs of the community, such as harvest of crops, demanded. Each subdivision selected its leader to be on the selectmen board, and Ken, despite his protestations, was elected by all as "speaker of the community." In fact, there was precious little change in what people were doing, because everybody was keenly aware that this small group might be the only people alive in the United States and Canada, and perhaps elsewhere.

The group agreed that this Thanksgiving would be extremely special. The weather was getting nasty, and Cheyenne Mountain had closed up for the winter. Eureka already had one super-cold snap, but it didn't last too long and to everyone's relief, the stream and the power station still worked.

Ken had asked for the Seneca V to make a shuttle run to Eureka because atmospheric conditions had become too rough for the Gossamer Phoenix, now stationed at Halcyon for the winter. Ken returned with a load of cargo without much explanation. Thus, as everyone crammed into the enlarged dinning hall, it was a total surprise when out came 14 large cooked turkeys, with cranberry sauce and bread stuffing. A cheer went up.

Ken explained, "We found a market in Rio Dell on our way back from the geysers. Although it was not burned, it had been looted, but the freezer room was still locked. Since it was under snow and in the permafrost zone, we broke open the lock and found a stock of turkeys and other meat – most of which we left there. More food and supplies remain there, but these were all the turkeys. I don't know how many more such repositories we may find, but we will keep looking. There were also, under a fallen shelf, a bunch of spices, frozen to the floor. We kept some at Eu-reka but the rest are now here.

The meal ended with a toast by Commander Pierce to the California "angels." He said, "I may be paraphrasing Churchill, but never have so many owed so much to so few. Thank you!"

19. THIRD HUMAN CONTACT

The weather reports from Cheyenne Mountain continued, since Halcyon had still not set up a receiving station with anything like Cheyenne Mountain's capabilities. The reports were showing slow improvement in temperatures. But notably, the persistent equatorial cloud was shrinking in latitude, and gaps could be seen in a band that included the extreme southern part of South America. Dissipation of the cloud layer would allow more solar heating and accelerate the transition to a warmer climate. The Earth still had a lot of fossil CO_2 that would help.

But on December 2, the Halcyon refugees heard an electrifying announcement from the people who remained at Cheyenne Mountain: "We have established ham radio contact with southern Chile. People there had picked up our transmission and built and modified their system to respond." No one left in Cheyenne

Mountain spoke Spanish, so the feed was transferred by the en-crypted ham radio signal to Eureka, where Maria, who is fully bilingual, responded.

On December 3, Ken and Maria made a report to the Halcyon and Cheyenne Mountain refugees. Ken summarized the satellite data and trends, and after reminding everyone that summer had almost arrived in Chile, Maria took over.

She said, "It appears that we are in contact with a group of six technicians and a visitor originally posted to a meteorological station on an island in far southern Chile, in the Chilean fjord region. Because of the persistently miserable weather, the station had been built out of reinforced concrete upslope from the ocean and sheltered behind a small mountain, with the instruments on the ridge above them in a small shack. Normally, a crew of six ran the station, including two husband-wife pairs and two children, with rotation to Chiloé Island every two weeks.

"Because Chile had an excellent tsunami and earthquake warn-ing system, partly a relic of the massive Puerto Montt earthquake, one of the worst ever seen, they received ample warning of the tsunami. The crew had climbed to the top of the ridge to see the tsunami, and thus were 2,600 feet above sea level when it came. The original wave was even higher, but the islands seaward broke up the flow into a confusing mess of clashing waves and riptides, extraordinarily violent but diminished in height and slowed in time. The station was inundated, but not really damaged structur-ally. The waves receded, and the crew returned to the station and watched in horror as the sun was blotted by an enormous cloud-bank that made daytime into a dim twilight. Then came a warn-ing of extreme cold, so the station prepared by bringing in wood.

"It seems the cold never got much lower than 5 degrees below zero F, but there were enormous storms on an almost continuous basis. Their stored food ran low, and they had to find some partially sheltered area to fish. Three days later, during a rare calm period, the crew of a fishing boat (a man with his wife, 16-year-old son, and 14-year-old daughter) came into the station after a harrowing journey. They had good fishing gear. Thus, they have lived almost exclusively on fish and seaweed for three years, with an occasional sea gull, and they have all lost a lot of weight. But they have recently begun seeing occasional breaks in the clouds, and the area's vegetation is regrowing as the temperature warms. About three months ago, the fishermen, husband, wife and their son tried to leave the island to get to their village on the mainland in what looked like a break in the weather. Almost within sight of shore, there were enormous rip currents, and the boat went down. Their daughter, Esmeralda, is heartbroken but alive," Maria paused.

Ken said, "It appears that the cold-adapted vegetation like the southern beech survived a cold that never got as extreme as what we experienced up here. Remember, the intense cold always came with clear skies and north or northeast wind from Canada, a continental land mass, but the skies in Chile were always cloudy."

"Finally," Maria said, "They pirated all the electronic equipment they had to make a ham radio a few weeks ago, but they had no electrical power. Fortunately some of the equipment ran on small solar panels, and these were hooked up and they finally got on the air. They were ecstatic to have made contact with us. However, while the ocean is quieting down a bit, it is still violent and they have no idea where to go to find more people. They are in no immediate threat of their lives, because fishing from shore is now easier. But without any boat, they are trapped on the island. The fisherman said there were wild cattle on the next island, and perhaps more people are there."

Ken closed the report. "Thank you, Maria. The comment that they have recovering vegetation is very good news. I have been down there, and the forests were dense and diverse. The comment about seagulls and wild cattle on the mainland is fascinating, and shows an ecosystem not nearly as badly trashed as the Northern Hemisphere. Also, the tsunami was not as large as that on the West Coast of the United States, and probably Asia. Regretfully, none of the trees I knew of had any fruits we could eat. I propose what we need from them more than anything is their meteorological data for the past three years, and what we can give them is news, music, and long-distance companionship. I propose that we establish a Spanish language program and transmit it on that frequency. Maria, could you survey the refugees and find two or three volunteers for this task?"

"Con mucho gusto!" she replied. No translation was needed.

The next day, Ken, Roger, Commander Pierce, the president, Jonathan, Andrew, and the chief of the Navy and Air Force pilots, and by radio, David, conferred for a planning session. The weather was cold but not bitter, almost always above freezing in daytime and usually no more than 22 degrees F at night. The question was what they should do about the Chilean contacts besides what they had decided yesterday.

The first question was whether or not that approach was in the best interest of the American and Chilean survivors. The answer was clearly "yes." But "how?" was another question. How, indeed?

The comments from Chile and the last information received before all communications ceased in the severe cold indicated that the oceans were still wracked with mammoth storms as the still-warm oceans, with their enormous heat capacity, battled with the cold air above them. No vessel the Americans had, or probably could reasonably build, would be able to survive these conditions. The Navy men demurred, viewing oceangoing capability as a challenge, and a hypothesis that had to be tested. Would flying to Chile be possible? If the Americans were able to get there, was there any way to land? Everyone went their own way and promised to return on the next day with proposals.

The next day, Ken had a long talk with the people remaining at Cheyenne Mountain about whether or not any land was showing above the clouds in the Andes. They responded that for the first two years nothing emerged. Recently, however, there had been many periods in which the highest peaks of the Andes appeared cloud-free, and there were now places in valleys at lower elevations that were almost always above the clouds. The persistent cloud cover usually extended no farther north than Isla de Cedros, off Baja California, Mexico. Inland in Mexico was a featureless snowfield, but thin coastal snow-free strips were present, especially at the northern end of the Sea of Cortez. Still, assuming a pilot could refuel at Isla de Cedros, the first of the above-cloud landing site possibilities was almost 3,000 miles south of there, across the length of Central America. Once there, a pilot could do about 1,000 hops to Mount Aconcagua above Santiago, and from there a round trip to a point above the meteorological station, assuming that fuel had been stockpiled. But to what purpose, if the Americans couldn't land?

When the group met again, they determined that the only viable method for such extensive travel was by sea. They discussed the type of ship that could handle repeated typhoon winds and seas, but the Navy men insisted that in the mid-ocean, waves were something that could be handled. Near shore, navigability was not at all certain.

The Colorado and California survivors decided that when spring came, both ships would sail south and aim for Isla de Cedros as an interim port for excursions into the storm zone. At the same time, the Eureka site would become a shipyard for larger ships designed for rough sea conditions. About half of the Navy people, despite being mostly pilots – not seafarers – would move to Eureka in the spring, while the others would help Andrew in scoping the southern explorations. The Air Force affiliates would stay at Halcyon and develop long-range aircraft – sailplanes on steroids – with super-efficient engines to allow very long flights. Turboprops were the chosen method, and they started to search for small jet engines that could be modified into turboprops.

20. THE COLD: YEAR 4

The slow amelioration of winter was first noticed in Eureka. By consent, the group defined severe cold as any period three days or more in which the minimum temperature was 50 below zero F or colder, to separate it from normal winter conditions. Any outdoor work at Cheyenne Mountain was completely shut down after November 25, while severe cold never reached Halcyon. Severe cold occurred in Eureka for a total of only 16 days during the winter of the fourth year, so work could go on as usual. The primary work performed during the winter months was building housing and support structures outside of the refuge. The group insulated the walls by filling them with whatever plastic garbage they could find, because they still had not discovered a supply of standard insulation such as glass wool. The ongoing lack of intact glass windows was a trial, but they framed windows in such a way that if glass were found, it could be installed. Also, finding suitable wood debris near the hospital in good enough condition for construction was becoming more difficult. As long as the roads were not too snow-covered, the Jeep was constantly going out on wood-scavenging expeditions and, by February, the building was essentially complete. The roof was made waterproof by the simple expedient of using solid lumber, lapped like a boat. The heating system used galvanized ducting, some of which was rescued from the destroyed parts of the hospital and the supermarket. The building would be ready for up to 24 people by spring. It was subdivided so families could have small apartments.

The last severe cold occurred on February 12, followed by the usual intense snowstorms in February and March, which were interspersed with rainstorms. While the coastal plain usually was a muddy mess, the snow didn't linger. Regretfully, the unprotected small test plots of grass from the geysers area did not survive the severe cold, but the blackberry vines, which were heavily mulched and protected, did. The waterwheel power station was increased in capacity.

As soon as the stabilized snow crust was re-established in March, the Jeep went out on three trips to the geysers, collecting mostly grass plugs. The places where plugs had been removed the previous year already had grown over, so the refugees harvested them more aggressively this time. Because about 120 acres were persistently snow-free, this was a tiny fraction of the grass needed to support the flocks of sheep. The area supported two types of grasses: native bunch grasses near the warm water, and Mediterranean grasses with their large seed heads that stuck in socks farther inland. The group collected both types, but far more of the latter because those grasses seemed to tolerate the cold better and were the first to move into the area that recently had been freed of snow. The group noted that the snow-free area this year was significantly larger than last year.

They spent some time noting the sheep diagnostics, and there were actually two flocks with home ranges about a quarter mile apart. They appeared to be thriving.

The weather stabilized in early April, which meant that rainstorms struck like clockwork every three to five days – even in Halcyon. In the intervals between storms, the Seneca V was shuttled to Eureka to transport the thousands of grass plugs. The sprigs from the previous year had survived the Halcyon winter well, and there were now sprouts between the plugs from last year's seed heads. Within a couple of years, the survivors would have a couple of acres under grass from just the limited plugs of last year. Much thought was given to the grass plugs, and almost 1,800 were dedicated to the critical sheep pastures, bringing it to about 12 acres, while a few hundred additional plugs were placed around the dwellings to make a lawn. More than 500 plugs, mostly native grasses, were widely dispersed around the area in which erosion was worst in order to start the process of stabilization. Erosion was still a problem, and the Arroyo Grande Creek was carrying a very large silt load, especially in spring, requiring constant cleaning of the irrigation ditches and the waterwheel power station.

The winter in Halcyon had been primarily dedicated to the construction of a large heated greenhouse, the effectiveness of which was compromised by the lack of glass windows for light. Movable panels were made to enable opening the greenhouse to the sun when conditions were warm. About 30 people were dedicated to planting thousands of plant seedlings in the greenhouse to get a jump on the short growing season.

The other winter project was building a school and starting regular classes. The task was daunting due to the almost complete lack of teaching staples, such as blackboards, paper, and other school supplies. But John had recruited six dedicated teachers, and the sense of normalcy was greatly enhanced by instituting a regular five-day school week. The bell that had been uncovered from a ruined building in Halcyon itself sounded the time for the entire community.

In mid-summer, the entire town went out and divided last year's grass plugs into three segments, one of which was left where it was, while the others were dispersed to the edges of the pasture, as it was now being called. From a distance, the area actually looked green.

The crew made some additions to the Good Ship Peter to expand its holding capacity. In early May, the Peter and the Paul set sail for the Channel Islands to collect additional eucalyptus shoots, because the ones planted the prior year were thriving. Most of the Navy people and other techs went north to Eureka to start the process of building an ocean-capable vessel. The new housing was ready – not exactly beautiful – but the weather was still cold. The people from Cheyenne Mountain were finally able to reclaim their outdoor buildings from the new snow. However, they were now requesting some additional labor in Eureka, because they didn't have enough people to clear the runway for the Seneca V. The very upper end of the runway was almost clear of snow, and they would work so that the slightly warmer summer conditions could melt it enough for the Gossamer Phoenix to land. It was time for some sort of Plan B for Cheyenne Mountain.

The first task was lumber, and with that the Eureka refugees had a real break. The tsunami had poured up the Mad River and swept through lumber mills, carrying the existing milled lumber inland with the flood. A large pile had ended up on the hillsides near the community of Korbel in Humboldt County, and with the warming conditions it was now partially free of snow. The Jeep could access some of these piles, and immediately most of the labor force moved to the area to salvage wood useful for the ship. The first task was to build a real bridge over the Mad River, and once that was done, the VW and Volt could also aid in at least shuttling people and food back and forth. By early July, a large pile of lumber, mostly redwood but with some Douglas fir, was stacked at the sheltered end of the bay near the refuge. They had decided to build a two-masted ketch about 100 feet long, but lacked any lumber large enough for the keel and the masts. In the wreckage of the lumber mill, they found two rotary saws and one enormous band saw for lumber shaping. These were moved with their motors to the shipyard, and power was supplied from the power station. However, when the power was flipped on, it almost stopped the waterwheel because the drain was so high. They decided to incorporate the Volt in the power station, running a belt from its rear tire to the rotary saw, and the power problem was solved.

Meanwhile, crews had found a tree of about the right size for the keel, and cut it down the old-fashioned way – with axes (and blisters). They dragged it to the shipyard and, with the labor of almost every able-bodied person at Eureka, pulled it across the

saw for the cuts. After the first cut, they had one smooth surface, which made subsequent milling easier. In about five hours,
a 100-foot-long keel piece was completed and pulled onto the
launching slip.

From that point, progress was rapid. In the bay they had discovered lots of rebar that had been uncovered by the low ocean
level, so ribs were nested into notches in the keel and fastened
with reinforcing bar pegs. The lumber crew found suitable lumber to construct the masts, and these were dragged to the site but
not sawn until needed. The problem of sails would be solved as
soon as the Seneca could land at Cheyenne Mountain, which had
a supply of parachutes with nylon rip lines from the Air Force.
By mid-August, the Gossamer Phoenix with its enhanced range
could make the trip in one hop, land at Cheyenne Mountain and,
with the staff, refuel and load up about 200 pounds of parachute
webbing. Before leaving, Jonathan helped clear more of the roadway for the Seneca. The Cheyenne Mountain staff appeared to
be tiring of their "ménage à trios" and asked for rotation. Upon
Honathan's arrival in Eureka, a new group was set up to make the
sails and the ropes for the rigging.

The weather was getting colder on September 1, but that wasn't
obvious from the celebration when the ship was launched. The
Navy was given the task of naming the ship, and they chose "The
Constitution." They built a crane and stepped the mast into place.
The standing rigging was still a problem, and steel cables and
power lines interwoven in a heterogeneous mix were somehow
made into a workable rig. It was not pretty, but it was strong. It
would have to be. On September 7, the good ships Peter and Paul
arrived at Eureka to be part of the flotilla (and save survivors,

if necessary). The Constitution was sailed back and forth in the Bay by its crew, headed by Captain Will Rogers, about the only Navy man from Cheyenne Mountain with any sort of sailing experience. After three days, and feeling far better about the boat's capabilities, the group decided that it was too light and needed ballast, so they filled the hold with a lot of lumber that would be taken to Halcyon. The plan to add engines to The Constitution was set into motion, but the completion would have to wait until the next year because so much more work was needed. Finally, on September 12, the flotilla left through the gap into the ocean at exactly the time the tide was slack, so no major surf was present. The view from shore was one of the best sights everyone had seen in months, as the newly built boat sailed south.

The Seneca V arrived and started shuttling people from Eureka to Halcyon for the winter. In two weeks, Eureka was back to its normal complement, and the salmon harvest was about to begin. Three weeks later, Maria and David, along with a large load of salmon, made the final winter flight to Halcyon, and they would stay until their wedding in November.

The arrival of the flotilla at Halcyon was an occasion of major celebration. Because the seas were calm, The Constitution's lumber was unloaded and unceremoniously dumped into the ocean to float ashore near the mouth of Arroyo Grande Creek. With almost 100 people helping, the lumber was collected and rapidly moved near the village where real wood was much appreciated. Then all three ships headed to the well-protected Port San Luis – their base for the upcoming winter. The time would be used to make a number of relatively minor changes in the rigging of The Constitution, based upon their experience on the way down.

While Thanksgiving lacked the turkeys of last year's blowout, it was still satisfying. Numerous frozen chickens had been found in a snowed-in market freezer, and what they lacked in size they made up in number. There was still no thought of harvesting from the growing flock, because the eggs were so welcome.

Ken and the meteorological teams, now greatly expanded, waited until a week after Thanksgiving to deliver bad news. The occasion was an all-day "State of the Planet" briefing, with input from Cheyenne Mountain data sources and the NCAR scientists now at Halcyon. Almost every discussion started with, "If I only had..." followed by some key data source, but the effort had to go on.

Ken started, "You may have noticed that the orange sunsets from the stratospheric sulfuric acid have not faded further. We are also seeing the rate of warm-up slowing. We have gone over the options, and have come to the conclusion that somewhere not in the Americas sulfur is being emitted high into the stratosphere from ongoing and violent volcanic eruptions. The most likely sources in our opinion are eruptions based on the splitting of Africa along the rift zone that was triggered by the impact. Contamination of the atmosphere with this additional sulfur has several possible consequences. First, the climate we have now may not get much better, and second, the equatorial clouds, nucleated on the mid-altitude sulfur emission, will persist along with their consequent global cooling. The good news here is that the cooling of the oceans is reducing the difference between air and water temperature. But the bad news is that this pattern was also most likely the cause of the most massive extinction of life on Earth – the Permian extinction when between 80 and 95 percent of all species were extinguished. The ocean was especially hard hit, probably going anaerobic and acidic due to the CO_2, essentially dissolving the shells of species relying on calcareous skeletons or shells, like coral, and sparing species like anemone. On land, it was not as bad, and the mammalian precursors were among the species that survived and later thrived. If it makes you feel any better, one of the models has the Earth reversing the present cooling and getting a lot warmer, even tropical.

"We have to accept the fact that we do not have enough data, and existing weather satellites will not last forever. Thus, I propose that some small fraction of our effort should be to begin global-scale observations with highly efficient aircraft, with analysis of the suspected rift volcanoes our first priority. We have several options: One is to go to Europe to look for pockets of survival there. From there we would fly over the eastern Mediterranean Sea, traverse the Middle East, continue in a southeasterly bearing and go down the coast of the Indian Ocean toward the point of impact, staying upwind of the plumes of the supposed volcanoes. Before that, however, we propose to try to access the European weather satellites that might still be operational.

"The weather satellites are supposed to stay in their geosynchronous orbits and beam down data continuously. But there is another mode – data stored on board and released upon interrogation. I am proposing that the Cheyenne Mountain group identify this capability, and gently nudge one of the weather satellite so that it moves equatorially to see Africa, take data, and then return and download here. I believe that we would need very limited data capture, perhaps one picture per hour, but that might be enough. It is certainly better than anything we have now.

"Finally, as The Constitution works its way under the cloud plume, I propose that in addition to the measurements taken, we should try to establish automated stations to beam back data. The Cheyenne Mountain XM uplink could be modified so that a subcarrier signal relays coded meteorological data that could be invaluable."

21. SOUTH INTO THE CLOUD

The Constitution was ready to go almost immediately. The sailing team had constructed livestock stalls in the hold in case they could catch some of the purported cattle. Since it was summer in the Southern Hemisphere, they all hoped the weather would be less violent than winter. The "Good Ship Peter" under Andrew and its all-student crew of four begged to go along at least as far as Isla de Cedros off Baja California, Mexico, the first proposed stopping point. The Peter, which was originally 36 feet long, had been lengthened, and the bow raised almost like a dory. The deck was completely covered, and the mast support of the sloop rigging reinforced with steel cables. Also added was a deep-ocean keel that could be pivoted down, greatly aiding stability and increasing speed by about 30 percent in a moderate wind.

Ken was of two minds, but told Andrew, "If you didn't have a wife and child here to come back to, I would never let you go. But you do, and they would miss you. So, go if you must, but be sage, be careful, and return!"

Thus, on December 11, both ships headed out into the deep ocean, as the Halcyon teams were working to protect crops from the first modest cold snap.

The question about the ability of the Peter to keep up was soon answered. With the keel down, the Peter was almost as fast as The Constitution in strong winds, and actually faster in light airs. It would not be a handicap, and the Navy crew was actually happy to have the company. The deep ocean was marked by large high waves that were not breaking until the approached shore, as though they came from some very distant storm. Since the winds were persistently abeam, the ships made good and steady progress, staying well out to sea, until finally making a southeast turn toward Isla de Cedros. The west shore was a welter of massive surf, and was unapproachable. But on the lee side, near the southeast corner, was a ruined jetty and small harbor, now rather shallow because the sea was about 11 feet lower than before the impact because of the massive snow and ice building up on any land away from an ocean.

The ships tied up together, and Andrew's group was well received and praised by the Navy folk. Food was exchanged and The Constitution crew was sad about having to leave the Peter behind. Andrew spoke for his entire crew of four. "We want to go the full distance with you. You have seen that we can keep up, and we have enough food without drawing from your stores, with a little fishing as we go. You might very well need a smaller vessel in the Chilean fjords, and we don't dare risk The Constitution inshore."

No decision was made that night, and because Will Rogers had no written instructions, he radioed Halcyon. Ken was not completely surprised, but when Will proposed his response, Ken accepted the plan. The logic of Andrew's arguments were compelling, if the waves near the equator were no worse than those seen to date. But no one knew what lay under the cloud deck. It could be overwhelming and defeat even The Constitution. The next morning Will said, "Ken and I agreed, but under one condition. You can come. But if I raise this red flag on my mast, it is because I think you would be in severe danger. Then home you go!"

"Agreed," said Andrew.

Later that morning, the crews moved out behind Isla de Cedros into the channel and experienced the first really strong swells. Both ships handled them well. Once they were out to sea, the sky gradually dimmed and as they looked south, it seemed awfully dark. They all felt a bit like Christopher Columbus sailing into the unknown and fearing the consequences. But the winds were about the same, and the waves, though large, were not breaking. The motion on the ships, especially the Peter, was a swooping twisting pattern, and two of Andrew's crew members were violently seasick. By 4:00 p.m., they were fully under the cloud, but the sea and waves hadn't changed. They had been warned about massive equatorial storms seen in Year 1 – one of the possible factors that could keep the equatorial cloudbank intact for years – but it wasn't the case. The air was cooler but, if anything, the wind dropped a bit. The Constitution was taking regular measurements of air and sea temperatures as they went. On they cruised in the murky half-light, and the sun set awfully early. Andrew had a simple compass and a radio set, but Will had put a red light on the mizzenmast, and it was a cheery presence and greatly aided navigation at night. By the next morning, they were well into the cloud deck, but the dreaded storms were not occurring. In a few days at this rate, they would reach the equator.

Well before they reached the equator, the winds dropped to gentle breezes. Their pace slowed significantly, but it was a lot better than typhoons. The ocean water was surprisingly cool, which probably mitigated the storms. The Constitution had good navigation capability, and every third day or so, the two vessels would pull alongside and exchange information and, occasionally, food. Fishing was good, and the crew of the Peter had caught a good-sized tuna. Daily reports were being transmitted to Halcyon, and hence to Eureka and Cheyenne Mountain. In return, they were passing progress reports on to Marcos, the key spokesperson in Chile. South of the equator, the winds reversed direction, blowing off the land, and the swells decreased markedly. The wind was cold, however. This pattern continued for the next two weeks until, as they approached the latitude of Santiago, Chile, the sea became rougher. A storm of gale-force winds whipped up, and Will hove The Constitution heading into the waves with a sea anchor and threw a line to the crew of the Peter, who tied on. For two days, they essentially held still until the winds abated. They then headed south again, making better progress in the freshening breeze. Three days later, the pattern occurred again, perhaps even stronger – a Class I typhoon. That too was ridden out. Afterward, the winds switched yet again and started blowing from the west. The waves had become much higher and powerful.

As the winds abated, The Constitution came alongside the

Peter, and Will said, "The GPS shows that we are only 39 miles from Isla Juan Fernandez, the island of *Robinson Crusoe* fame. Our report is that there are no reefs along the leeward side, which has a protected harbor. I am interested in what survived on these ocean islands since it could not have been super-cold out here. Stay close. By the way, last night in the dark we passed Isla San Felix which, according to our maps, has a long runway built as a possible landing site for a Space Shuttle in distress. There is also one on Easter Island."

In only a few hours islands appeared to the south, still shrouded in the perpetual cloud that was so depressing. The waves were very large from the west, but as the boats came around the southeast a beautiful harbor appeared well protected. The mariners anchored, and Will went aboard the Peter and a small crew headed ashore. As they expected, everything below about 1,500 feet elevation had been swept clear, but unexpectedly they found abundant new plant growth. Higher up on the hills, they could see trees, even coconut palms. No people were around, but numerous sea gulls were gracefully circling in the sky, alighting on the ground, and squawking loudly. Everyone wanted to capture some and bring them back to Halcyon, but this was not the time. Coming back to the boat, they saw what looked like logs on the beach. Looking closer, they realized it was a large herd of southern elephant seals sprawled out on the beach to get whatever warmth the sky delivered. The crew took photos. The people in Halcyon were delighted to learn that the oceanic islands had this much life. An automated meteorological station was left on a point of land well above the wave line.

Moving out to sea, they approached the coast where the

meteorological station was located. It was about as nasty a sea as one could imagine, with big waves crashing ashore. However, they were in radio contact, and Marcos said to go about six miles south and enter a passage that was sheltered. They were then instructed to come up behind the island on the southeast side. Marcos gave careful directions about avoiding hazards, and they stayed on line during the entire maneuver. The Peter went first, sounding as it went, and eventually they could see the lee side of the island. However, they encountered a massive tidal rip, enhanced by wave action, and so they once again paused.

Marcos said, "The tide shifts in three hours and 20 minutes. There will be no more than 20 minutes of slack water, so move quickly."

The next three hours were miserable because the boats were barely under weight, and pitched and bobbed like corks on the waves. Finally, Marcos said, "Start now, and keep that tree on the spit as your target. There is a barely sheltered cove under its lee, and deep water right up to shore. We will be there."

Moving through a sea of ocean foam where the tides and waves had raged not 20 minutes earlier was a bit eerie, but they were well into shore before the tide started to change, and with it a bore-like standing wave. They were tied up by then. The greetings were unrestrained and heartfelt, and all were led up to the shack in which what passed as a feast was laid out. Rock lobster, some thin slices of seagull meat, and mussels steamed in seaweed, to which William added blackberry preserves on biscuits cooked on their wood stove.

Both crews wanted to sleep on their boats in case something came up. To their delight, what came up the next morning was weak sunshine in a washed-out blue sky with enough brightness to cast shadows. Instantly the colors were richer, the waves bluer, and Will brought out eggs for breakfast. He thought it would be a big deal, and Marcos' family and workers were appreciative, but in fact they had been routinely raiding sea gull nests for eggs for years. Still, the chicken eggs did taste better. And again, biscuits, and gravy.

The rest of the day was spent planning how to set up the automated weather station. It was actually quite complete, with data from all the usual components cached and then downloaded to XM radio once per day. It included sensors for direct and diffused sunlight, pH measurements for rain, and a number of other systems. It was solar powered and should last for many years.

The next task was conducting a survey of the existing villages in the fjord region, aboard the Peter because it was more nimble. Again, the crew waited for the slack tide moment, and passed into the sound behind the barrier islands. The vegetation had been stripped up to about 1,000 feet, but above that was a dense forest, and then snow at about 2,500 feet. The gulls followed the boat and Andrew said, "We have got to get some of those back to Halcyon, and not to eat."

For three days, they coursed along the protected reaches of the sound with Marcos as their guide. They visited three villages, which all had been swept from the land as though they had never existed. In one, a forlorn small church stood on a hill just above where the waves had swept away the village. It was already falling into ruin, sort of weeping for its lost flock. When the seas looked too rough, they had to turn back. Marcos became more and more morose as he realized the extent of the damage. As they approached, Marcos pointed out animals on a hill. Wild cattle. He said, "There used to be a farm on that island, but it is gone."

Back at the base, Will, a confirmed carnivore, was all for getting the cattle as soon as possible. Everyone missed dairy products, and so consensus was reached. They sailed The Constitution across the slack water with the Peter, and both tied up without incident at a small cove that Marcos said had been the site of the farm. The cattle that they saw on the hillside were skittish and ran away. Marcos mentioned that a point on the northeast coast could act as a pen, if the crews could drive them there. So they formed a line from the snow line to the shore and moved slowly toward the cattle. The cattle clearly did not like going in the snow, and moved in the opposite direction. As the land narrowed, the people at the snow line could go onto dry land and eventually reached the north shore of the island. The cattle still had not been spooked as the crews slowly pushed them toward the spit. The line got tighter and suddenly one young bull moved toward the line but held back when two people waved their arms and yelled. Now the herd was more animated, but it still moved toward the spit. The line closed up, and the cattle were confined to about an acre on the shore, with no way off but through the herders' line or swimming.

Andrew ran back and brought the Peter right onto the shore near the cattle. Marcos now broke out the fishing nets, and three people moved toward the herd. A relatively small animal bolted from the herd, hit water, and tried to swim past the line. It was easily captured and carried onto the Peter and tied to the mast. Two more were selected and removed from the herd, and then the Peter, with three cattle aboard, headed back to the cove where

The Constitution was tied up. They lowered the animals into the stalls in The Constitution's hold and back went the Peter to the island farm. By evening, they had a mixed herd of eight animals – three bulls and five heifers – in the hold. Then came the hard work – two days of collecting grass – some fresh, mostly dried – and some seaweed to feed the beasts on the long journey home. The Constitution looked like a hay barge, and even the Peter was carrying some of it. Finally, at Andrew's insistence, they collected 12 seagulls (of unknown sex) and put them in a makeshift cage. They would be fed garbage scraps.

Marcos, his wife Rosa, and other Chileans had very few personal items at their remote meteorological station, other than clothes. But there was one item of immense importance – the station's meteorological log. In addition, Esmeralda carried a statue of the Virgin Mary, protector and patroness of the met station, and lovingly placed it into the captain's cabin in the Peter.

The ships were riding low as they set sail through the slack tidal rip, south to the pass, and then north. The only real trouble came during a gale when water washed over parts of The Constitution's deck, soaking the grass that was starting to go bad in any case. By 10 days, they had moved north almost to the equator, but the livestock had by then eaten all the grass. The dried hay and seaweed seemed to last longer, and was rationed so it would run out the day before they landed. They sent word to the people in Halcyon that these cattle were going to stress their resources. Happily, it was spring in Halcyon by now, and the Paul sailed to start to harvest the seaweed that would perforce be cattle feed, with grazing in grass for only four hours every third day. The cattle were looking stressed but none had died when they finally arrived at Port San Luis. A spring storm was acting up, so they had to quickly dock and unload the cattle for the overland trip to Halcyon.

Despite the daily reports that the ship crews had been sending, the arrival of the ships was a cause for joyous celebration. The seagulls were released, and immediately found food galore among the rocks near the port. Their cries were a welcome addition to the too-quiet environment.

By the next day, the cattle were at Halcyon and were given time on the grass and the even more abundant willow shoots on the creek bank. That night, they were herded into the makeshift barn and fed seaweed. Andrew and the sailors marveled at how fast the grass was spreading. From the boats, the shore near Halcyon looked green with willows in the creek edge and the grass farther north. There also was considerable willow growth near the mouth of the Santa Maria River farther south.

This scene lasted about three days until the crew realized that the herd was tearing up the grass roots with their heavy hooves on the soft earth. A new pen was made in sandy soil closer to the ocean, but still with some willows. Any grass was cut as it grew by the livestock team of four people, all of whom had prior animal experience on farms. Two of the heifers had just had calves and were still providing milk. The first butter, from cream shaken (not stirred) was a delight.

Marcos and the Chileans were taken to Eureka in one of the Peter's shuttles, and decided they actually liked it better than Halcyon because it more closely approximated their prior environment. They immediately were added as a most welcome addition to the small fishing team, and one of the two new boats being built was assigned to them. By now, the ocean level was no longer dropping, and the reeds were making a well-defined demarcation of the bay. With the help of the refugees and the abundant sawn lumber, the Chileans built three houses near the pier, and their skills soon increased both the types and amount of fish caught.

Once the Chileans were settled, the Eureka team made another run to the geysers and, with the aid of a towed toboggan, they brought back seven sheep from each flock – one ram and six ewes. Far more were left at the site. One flock was to exist at the refuge, where there was a growing pasture, but both flocks were kept there for the next month until the resources at Halcyon, strained by the cattle, could improve. The grass had to be protected, however, in winter when the occasional severe colds occurred. But otherwise, in spring, it was thriving and spreading. In a month, the other flock was sent south to Halcyon. Unlike the cattle, the sheep worked well with the pasture because their hooves didn't tear up the grass. Thanks to all the willow shoots, the sheep took care of themselves. The whole scene was becoming bucolic.

Thousands of seedlings harvested from the previous year resulted in thriving agricultural fields, with the plants far more advanced than in the previous spring. Hope was that some of them would finally set seed. During the excursions toward San Luis Obispo, Jeanette found an apple orchard under only minimal snow cover, and a group dug up more than 120 trees and moved them to the south-facing ridge above Halcyon. Finally, deep in Cheyenne Mountain food stores, the refugees found a series of large sealed containers with unmilled winter wheat. One was shipped to Halcyon and would, if it were still viable, allow

Halcyon to start plantings of winter wheat, well-suited to the local climate.

Andrew and The Constitution made a run down to Santa Rosa Island, harvested many hundreds of eucalyptus shoots, some grass plugs, and shrubs, and brought them back to Halcyon. The island ecosystems, limited as they were, were saving the day. There was a real sense of having turned a corner.

Ken was sitting on one of the crude "lawn" chairs that people had thrown together with whatever waste wood was available. Cathy was returning from the fields. Her hair was a mess, her clothes tattered and dusty, her hands coarse, and fingernails broken. Ken thought she was the most beautiful vision a man could have. She came up, and dumped herself in his lap as they used to do, but in recent days, months, years, things had been so desperate, so busy.

"Hi, beautiful," Ken said, and despite her sunburn, Cathy blushed.

22. FOURTH HUMAN CONTACT

By mid-summer of Year 4, the Cheyenne Mountain group had been seamlessly melded with the California refuges, and the Chileans were thriving in Eureka. The monthly town meetings showed progress on all fronts, including new pastureland being developed among the willows near the mouth of the Santa Maria River, a few miles south.

At the end of the meeting, new business was taken up. The exploration teams had a suggestion. A trip to Europe would be a very difficult undertaking, and could not be attempted until improvement of weather next summer. With the Seneca and The Constitution both highly capable, it was time to consider the trip.

Ken began, "The data from the southern trip showed that the Pacific islands appear to have survived the cold, and their ecosystems were recovering. We now have the ability to go to one of the most important Pacific islands that, as it happens, also lie just north of the equatorial cloud deck. The Hawaiian Islands may well have survivors, and in the last month of summer, I think we should try to travel there rather than to Europe. I propose that the Gossamer Albatross, maxed out with fuel and cameras, make the round trip within two weeks, while The Constitution and Peter go out to sea and act as lifeguards should anything happen to the Albatross. If contact is made, The Constitution and Peter will then continue to the islands to follow up on the sitings."

The discussion was intense and detailed, but consensus was rapidly made to scrap a proposed excursion to the Alaskan Islands by The Constitution, and instead focus on Hawaii.

It was the last week of August before everything was ready, and the upgraded Gossamer Albatross took off with the current chief pilot, Ben Halsey, at the controls. He launched before dawn so he would have enough time to survey the area and return before dark, although a night landing was a real probability and preparations were made for flares at the airport should they be needed.

The Constitution was now more than 1,000 miles out, accompanied by the Peter, and the Albatross flew directly over them and checked radio contact. The crew decided to go first to the island of Hawaii – by far the largest and with the most land areas above the tsunami's reach. It was already after noon when the Albatross sighted the Mauna Loa and Kilauea volcanoes, with modest low-altitude smoke plumes coming from both. Even the snow on Mauna Kea had a dark patch that may have been a small eruption, but it was now quiet. The most striking feature was the heavy blanket of snow that extended down to roughly an altitude of 3,000 feet. The devastation line of the tsunami was clearly visible high on the island shores, at least several thousands of feet above sea level, and almost to the snow line. The coastal zones were swept clean, but there was a persistent haze of green at elevations from sea level to perhaps 1,000 feet. Ben was thrilled at the sight, which was by far the most green he had seen in four years, and he radioed back the message. The radios were abuzz with joyous responses. He spotted a small region above the tsunami line and below the snow that seemed to have intact vegetation of some sort, but it was all brown. Even far from the volcanic peaks, large streaks of black lava extended down and through the prior site of Hilo and into the ocean, at least three miles wide, while farther to the southeast other narrower streaks reached to the sea, the latter probably from Kilauea.

Flying to the southeast corner of Hawaii, the Albatross dropped to about 1,000 feet and started northwest along the shore. The island appeared green everywhere near the shore between the lava streams. Clearly, vegetation had survived the tsunami and was regrowing without the threat of bitter cold at mainland sites. While some large trees or bushes were evident, it looked more like a grassland.

Ben sounded excited when he said, "Near where Hilo used to be, I see signs of crude buildings in a grid pattern along a street, and what appear to be trees carefully aligned in the grid. There is a small pier, and what appear to be canoes. I am dropping down lower, and I see people running out and waving. There is an American flag flying at one building. I will circle and drop the contact package – including a radio and enough batteries to last a few days."

Ben checked the wind direction, which appeared to be a trade wind from the east, and jettisoned the parachuted package just over the shore so it would drift inland to the village. With a final wing wag, Ben continued northwest, alerting the ships of the location, which did not appear to have a harbor. The Peter would be useful here. As he flew along the coast, he saw no further evidence of survivors.

Ben was halfway to Maui when the radio crackled to life. A voice said, "Are we ever happy to see you. We have no idea what has been happening after the earthquake, tsunami, volcanic eruptions, bitter cold, and three years of cloud cover, but we thought we night have been the last people alive on Earth. We are survivors from the National Park Service Hawaiian Volcano Observatory at Kilauea and the small town of Volcano, plus about 100 others who were high enough to survive the tsunami. We fled down the mountain to avoid the eruptions, and then were driven down to sea level by the cold. We have a few plants, including a very few trees that seem to be able to survive the new conditions – mostly from people's backyards – fish in modest numbers, and canned goods from the wreckage of stores. We have not had a chance to read all your materials, but now that we have a radio, please tell us what is next? We fear that we are running out of food and can't grow enough to survive without the dwindling supply of canned food."

Ben keyed in, "Welcome! We are very happy to find you. We represent a small group of catastrophe survivors located in California, along with a group broadcasting on XM satellite radio from Colorado. We have two ships that are halfway to Hawaii, and they will now initiate contact with you by radio. By our estimates, your group constitutes about half of the entire population of the United States, and the greenery on your island is vastly more extensive than anything we have seen on the mainland. I have to continue the survey of Maui, then fly back, with my limited fuel supply. If you can find both a flat road that is 1,000 feet long and gasoline from ruined service stations, we could in the future land and refuel."

Crossing to Maui, Ben made landfall at about the site of the Hana Ranch. Again, he saw vegetation of some sort, perhaps grasses, and above that, the snow-covered Haleakala volcano. "Cattle," Ben exclaimed, "and a lot of them. And now I see huts scattered around Hana Bay. People are running around and staring at me. They seem far more reserved than at Hilo."

However, no one in their wildest optimism had planned for finding two groups, and thus there was no contact package to drop. Ben hauled out a note pad and wrote, "A ship will arrive in a week from California, and there are also survivors on Hawaii," and he tied it on a scarf. Coming in very low, he cast it just inland, wagged his wings and then climbed to cruising altitude. The Constitution came on immediately. "We are on our way, and the Peter will again be vital to get ashore at Hana Bay, which is shallow."

Ken came on from Halcyon, saying, "I am intrigued that the orchard and village at Hilo were laid out on a neat grid, while the dwellings at Hana are scattered. The former looks like federal planning, now confirmed by radio, while the latter seems more native Hawaiian. What good news in both cases."

The Albatross then set off on the long flight back to Halcyon, success in hand.

Three weeks later, The Constitution arrived back at Halcyon with two Hilo families, including the chief staff scientist from

Hawaii Volcanoes National Park. It was clear that considerable resources were available in Hawaii from the growing grasslands, especially if enhanced by some cattle from Hana. But they needed trees more suitable to New England than Hawaii, especially the newly discovered apple trees from San Luis Obispo. Further, the current Hilo climate should allow the growth of many plants currently growing at Halcyon, including the newly found winter wheat if it proved viable.

There was a certain aloofness from the Hana survivors – all of Hawaiian descent. They viewed the disaster as a way to reclaim their lost heritage. However, they were aware that the forms of sustenance of the original Polynesian settlers were now irrelevant in the new climate, and they needed resources. It was clear that they would view themselves as an independent country called Maui with trading arrangements with the Americans.

A week later, a town meeting was held at Halcyon, with Eureka, Cheyenne Mountain, Hilo, and Hana participating via ham radio. The crew of the Peter, now at Hilo, was online, too. They agreed that one-half of the sheep flock at Eureka, where survivors still had difficulty trying to keep enough grass growing during occasional cold snaps, would be translocated to Hilo. Concurrently, Maui would trade some cattle to Hilo in return for fruiting trees from both Halcyon and Hilo. Two members of the 54-person Hana village would go to Halcyon for basic medical training, and would return to Hana next year with medicines, while a few cattle would be shipped to Halcyon to improve their herd. The Halcyon cattle herd was by now entirely at the Santa Maria area, with the wreckage of the small town of Guadalupe as the local resource site.

23. CODA

Far to the east and south, a new doom was evolving. The entire continent of Africa had split along the pre-existing weakness at the African Rift Valley. Massive volcanoes, some now more than 20,000 feet high, extended almost all the way from the Afar Depression (now lava filled) near the Red Sea to Zimbabwe. Their continuous emissions of sulfur and ash had constantly reinforced the equatorial cloudbank, but their vigor was starting to fade as the basalt at their roots found a new way to escape. The crust had broken more than 3,600 miles in length, and highly fluid basalt was pouring out in amounts unprecedented in millions of years. It had taken three years to fill the Rift Valley and its great lakes with lava, and then it began crawling across the East Africa plains in waves as much as 1,000 feet thick.

By now, the incredible tropical rain forests of Africa, South

America, and southern Asia were nothing but a memory, killed by cold, darkness, and sulfuric acid in the rain. The three-year journey of lava from the African Rift Valley to the Indian Ocean was about to end in cauldrons of steam that signaled a conflict between ocean and land with vast consequences. The very least would be floods of sulfuric and hydrochloric acid aerosols from the lava-ocean interface emitted into the lower and middle troposphere. The rains would soon be even more poisonous, killing any seeds or shoots that might try to grow from the wreckage of the forests. The long and disastrous trials of the Earth's equatorial regions were about to get even worse.

Far to the north, in a bunker deep in the Ural Mountains, a decision from the army general in charge and his subordinates had been promulgated. For the 123 members of the top-secret Division 1 of the 31st Rocket Army, Urals Military District, food is running out. The division was designated to execute a second-strike mission from its deeply buried stronghold in the southern Ural Mountains, where it hosts seven SS 18 MIRV ICBMs – each with five 750-kiloton warheads. Their mission was to survive a U.S. first strike, and still be able to obliterate a large number of urban targets in the United States. While they have electric power from a small nuclear reactor buried deep underground, they are hopelessly trapped in unprecedented snow depths and contending with brutal cold, and they will all be dead from starvation within a few months, because the food supply was originally designed for a maximum three-year stay. Thus, it was decided by the Directorate that most of the team members would commit suicide so as to leave a small team able to endure two more years on the existing food supply.

But first, monitoring XM radio has revealed to them that U.S. military personnel are surviving in the well-known United States Cheyenne Mountain facility, which has been part of the old Soviet first-strike priority targeting since long before the catastrophe. Further, Cheyenne Mountain appears to be having success translocating some of their people from their icy prison, although it has become clear that the process is slow and difficult. They are moving to a place named "Halcyon," but no city of that name can be found on old Soviet maps. Thus, it is probably a code name for a coastal site in California.

Cheyenne Mountain, however, is obviously the technical heart of the U.S. survival and the source of the XM broadcasts, and it can and must be obliterated. It has taken almost a year to clear the launch pads to prepare them for seven missiles, each with five multiple-targeted, 1-megaton warheads. The Russians have decided to launch one of them aimed at Cheyenne Mountain, while the other four are fired on trajectories toward likely California coastal sites that might be "Halcyon" – one for Santa Barbara, two for Los Angeles (Santa Monica and Long Beach), and one for San Diego. In all cases, the multiple warheads would be spaced out enough to obliterate the entire coastal area. The last two missiles would be reserved for future launches, should a target become known.

Once the missiles are launched, the Cheyenne Mountain XM feed will be hijacked so that the Soviet national anthem can play for the last time for all to hear.

The date and time of launches have been set for the anniversary of the Bolshevik revolution, the 25th of October in the old Julian calendar, November 7 on the current calendar.

Tomorrow.

ABOUT THE AUTHOR

Thomas A. Cahill, Ph.D., is a
professor of physics at the University
of California, Davis. His early
work at UCLA, in France, and in
Davis, California, was in nuclear
physics and astrophysics, but he
soon began applying physical
techniques to applied problems,
especially air pollution. His data in
1973 on the impacts of airborne
lead was instrumental in the final
establishment of the automotive
catalytic converter in California in
1976. He proposed and supported
the law to lower sulfur in gasoline

Thomas Cahill at the World Trade Center
site in 2002. Photo by Sylvia Wright.

in 1977. He spent the following 20 years designing, building, and
running the aerosol network to protect atmospheric visibility at
U.S. national parks and monuments – now the national IMPROVE
program. In 1994, he founded the UC Davis DELTA Group to work
in two areas – aerosols and global climate change – for the National
Science Foundation (NSF) and the National Oceanic and Atmospheric
Administration (NOAA). Additionally his group analyzed aerosols
and human health impacts for the California Air Resources Board,
American Lung Association, and the Health Effects Task Force for
Breathe California of Sacramento Emigrant Trails. Because of this
health-related work, a U.S. Department of Energy colleague asked
Cahill and his team to evaluate air at the excavation project following
the collapse of the World Trade Center towers in the autumn of 2001.
Cahill was one of the first to warn that workers at the site were at risk
of serious health threats from the toxic metals in the air they were
breathing at the site. Cahill's first novel, *Annals of the Omega Project –
A Trilogy*, was published in the summer of 2012. *Ark: Asteroid Impact*
is the first in the *Ark* trilogy series.

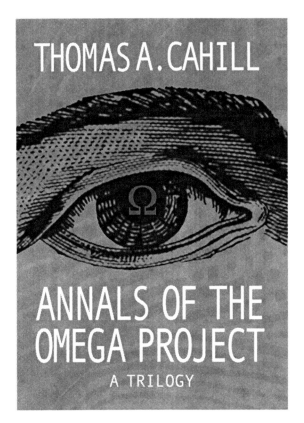

Thomas A. Cahill's first novel, **Annals of the Omega Project – A Trilogy** (ISBN: 978-1-937317-03-4), is a sci-fi thriller involving a UC professor and a group of psychic students calling themselves the "Omega Project." They formed their alliance to battle evil Coven members who invoke horrifically lethal "feedings" on the minds of their telepathic victims.

This 352-page book, published by EditPros LLC, is available in both print and digital (e-book) form through Amazon, Barnes and Noble, and other online book sellers.

EditPros LLC, Davis, California, USA · www.editpros.com

CPSIA information can be obtained at www.ICGtesting.com
Printed in the USA
BVOW011808200113

311122BV00001B/35/P